Cook, Code,

and a

Leap of Faith

Book 2 of the Garden Valley Series.

(Each book may be read independently or as part of the series.)

Lisa Buffaloe

Cook, Code, and a Leap of Faith

Visit the author's website at https://lisabuffaloe.com.

Cover Design: JoAnn Durgin

ISBN: 978-1-957715-62-9 (eBook)
ISBN: 978-1-957715-61-2 (Paperback)
ISBN: 978-1-957715-63-6 (Hardcover)

Cook, Code, and a Leap of Faith

Can a chef with a wounded past and a tech genius find hope, healing, and love in a small Tennessee town?

Sarah Livingstone has spent her life running from her mother's chaos, from heartbreak, and from believing she's worthy of a fresh start. When she lands a job at Rosie's Restaurant in Garden Valley, she hopes her culinary skills will finally open the door to belonging.

Peter Edwards, a brilliant AI programmer, is new to town and searching for more than just career success. But even as he codes solutions by day, Peter is searching for connection, meaning, and a love as genuine as the family he cherishes.

As their worlds collide, Sarah and Peter must confront old wounds and daring new dreams. Together, can they discover that sometimes the best recipes for love and faith are the ones you never planned?

A heartwarming story of second chances, found family, and the courage to take a leap of faith.

Table of Contents

Chapter 1

Morning sunlight streamed through the kitchen window as Sarah Livingstone methodically kneaded the dough.

Pausing, she gazed at the Smoky Mountains trees showing off their springtime colors. In the six months she'd been staying at her relative's house in Garden Valley, Tennessee, the rolling hills continued to fill her with a much-needed sense of peace and stability.

Hurried footsteps echoed in the hallway. "You can't shoot him."

"Yes, I can."

"But what will people say?"

"I won't kill him, just wing him. He'll be fine." With a cheerful grin, Sarah's aunt Dot entered the kitchen with her husband, Ulysses, trailing behind. "Good morning, Sarah. How are you on this lovely day?" Sarah's petite relative, with her short, wavy black hair, radiated mischief as she walked toward her.

Sarah chuckled at the mystery writer couple. "I'm better than whoever you're planning to shoot."

Dot waved a dismissive hand. "A bullet wound will play on the reader's sympathy for our main character. Besides that, what good would a mystery be without mysterious happenings?"

"Alright. You win this time." Sarah's uncle huffed. "But I will not be your stand-in when you practice. The last time you used me for your victim, you almost smothered me to death with that pillow."

Dot grinned as her eyelashes dramatically batted at her big and burly husband. "How else would I know how long our main character had to hold one over his victim's face before he died?"

"I'm hiring a bodyguard," Ulysses muttered.

"You'll be fine." Dot wrapped her arms around him. "I would never hurt you. I love you. Besides that, you're far too valuable to the writing process."

"At least I'm good for something." Ulysses' lips seemed to wrestle trying not to smile before he grinned and kissed her. "And I love you, too."

"And we love you," Dot said as she smiled at Sarah.

"Love you both, too. Even if you both live in an alternate world." It still amazed Sarah that her Christian relatives wrote best-selling mysteries without getting too graphic or gory.

Ulysses and Dot Franks weren't really her aunt and uncle, more like first cousins once removed or related in some way, but they still preferred being called aunt and uncle. And for that, Sarah was grateful. They were closer to her than anyone else.

Dot tilted her head as she studied Sarah. "It must be hard to be a nonwriter without characters running around in your head all day."

"I have enough difficulties controlling my thoughts as it is. I'm sticking to cooking and baking."

"We appreciate all you do for us," Ulysses said as he patted his stomach. "I've gained five pounds since you were kind enough to move in with us. You're an amazing chef."

"Thank you. I appreciate you two taking me in." Sarah rolled the dough out, cut it into strips, placed them on parchment-lined sheets, and lightly brushed the tops with melted butter.

"Taking you in?" Dot stared at her as if she were out of her mind. "We've been praying for you and begging you for years to come to stay with us. We would have adopted you at birth if your mom had let us."

Sarah swallowed hard. How different her life would have been if a kind, loving couple had raised her.

Dot stood next to her. "A little more cinnamon and sugar makes everything better."

Sarah shot a side-eye at her aunt. "I wish that were true."

"Well, maybe it *is* true," Dot said with a mischievous glint in her eyes. "If we'd sprinkled cinnamon and sugar like fairy dust on a few people, maybe things would have turned out differently."

"I'm not sure there are enough sweets in the world to change some people." Nothing could change her messed-up past. Her mother, Heather, was constantly moving from one relationship to the next. Sarah never fit in at the different schools and towns, always feeling secondary to Heather's current lover.

At least Heather had defended Sarah against men who tried to take advantage of her. Not that her mom was protective; Heather was just jealous and didn't want any man to notice anyone but her.

"I'd like to fling something more substantial at a few people," Dot grumbled.

"Probably best you didn't live closer. I wouldn't have wanted to bail you out of jail."

"I've been bailed out before," Dot said with a casual shrug.

"What?" Sarah forced her open mouth closed. She knew her aunt had a reputation for being ornery, but this was a new twist. "Care to share that story?"

"Just a small misunderstanding. Let's just say those songs about women getting back at their men who cheat have nothing on me."

A nervous chuckle came from Ulysses. "Good thing that wasn't me."

Sarah glanced back and forth between them. "Oh my goodness, don't stop there. I want to hear what happened."

Dot gave a sly smile. "You're too young."

"I'm twenty-four."

"That's what I mean. Maybe when you're thirty. Besides that, anyone who messes with us, we write into a novel and kill off. Your old boyfriend, who broke your heart, got off way too easily. He will be dealt with appropriately in our next novel — in a slow, painful way." Dot picked up a knife and slowly twirled it. "But don't worry, the name will be changed to protect his guilty, slimy hide."

The memory of her ex-boyfriend tightened a knot in Sarah's chest. She should never have trusted him. "I look forward to reading that novel."

"Now that you're staying in Garden Valley." Dot's eyes twinkled. "Since that big tech company moved into our area, there should be plenty of available men."

"I don't want someone just because they're available." Sarah placed her dough in the baking pan, slid it into the hot oven, and turned on the timer. She never wanted to be like her mom, who dated anyone and everyone as long as they were extremely wealthy.

"I know what you're thinking. You are *not* your mom, and you never will be. We'll keep praying for her."

Sarah rolled her eyes. "Praying for Mom doesn't help." She'd tried for years, and that hadn't done a thing.

"Never give up hope," Dot said. "Nothing is impossible for God."

Not wanting to get into another God discussion with her relatives, Sarah pasted on a polite smile, took the mixing bowls, and placed them in the sink. She couldn't wash away her past, but she could clean the kitchen.

"Can we help?" Dot asked.

"No, you two go back to your story world. Breakfast will be ready soon."

Dot patted Sarah's arm. "We appreciate you doing the cooking for us."

"It's the least I can do since you're letting me stay here for free," Sarah said.

Ulysses peered in the oven window. "With the scrumptious food you feed us, we should be paying you. How are things going at the restaurant?"

"Good. Rosie's is a great place to work." Sarah continued washing up the items. "The people are nice, but being a waitress isn't really what I want to do long term."

"You need to tell Rosie about your work experience and your recipes," Dot said. 'You have an amazing talent for cooking and baking."

"But I'm not a chef or a baker. I don't have any credentials." Sarah rinsed the bowl with a quick splash and then wiped it dry. Working on new recipe ideas relaxed her and gave her the chance to let the world's problems fade away, but that wasn't the same as attending culinary school.

"You don't need a diploma to prove you're good at what you do," Dot said. "You've worked in restaurant kitchens around the country. Take some of what you made yesterday and what you're making today to Rosie, along with your recipe book, and let her decide."

"You don't think that's presumptuous?"

"Of course not. If I were the owner of a restaurant, I'd be open to anyone who would help bring in more customers." A mischievous gleam flickered in Dot's eyes. "Besides that, what do you have to lose?"

Sarah stared out the kitchen window. Could she be a chef without professional training?

If she didn't try, she'd never know. What if her recipe ideas really were liked? Excitement rose inside her. Maybe, just maybe, she'd have an opportunity to really do what she'd always wanted.

Even though he'd been told the area was safe with a low crime rate, Peter Edwards locked the front door of his cabin. He couldn't imagine leaving his home open. People might not be a problem, but he didn't want to make it easier for a bear or raccoon to get inside. He was okay with animals like dogs and cats. Wildlife could stay in the wild.

Adjusting his glasses, Peter turned to admire the view of the grassy meadow bordered by the gently rising Tennessee mountain landscape. He never imagined at twenty-six that he'd be able to afford a log cabin with a stone fireplace, three bedrooms, and two baths. He had room for his master bedroom, an office, and a guest room for when his family visited. In addition, the five acres included a small barn, a pond fed by a deep spring, and a creek that softly wound along the property's rear boundary.

Peter chuckled to himself. His internal monologue, mirroring his realtor parent's language, made it evident that he should find something more to do with his time than work.

He got behind the wheel of his old Jeep and traveled the fifteen miles of winding roads to Garden. He hadn't planned on ever leaving his perfect idyllic family in Lexington, Kentucky. However, when a headhunter called with an opportunity for a once-in-a-lifetime, high-paying AI position at SAU Tech, Peter jumped at the chance.

Not only did he get a great occupation, he also got to work alongside his college best friend.

God had blessed him with a dream job, a fantastic home and property, and if his prayers were answered, he'd also get a perfect family just like the one he grew up in.

This time, when he found someone to date, he'd be careful to find a woman who'd been raised by a wonderful family like his and didn't have baggage like his old girlfriend.

.

Chapter 2

Sarah's palms were damp against the restaurant's cool, shining steel work surface. "You really like it?" she whispered, barely trusting her own voice.

"Yes. I love what you've made." Rosie Rodriguez stood beside Sarah. Elegant and composed, Rosie carried herself with quiet confidence. Her long black hair, glossy save for a few graceful streaks of silver, was swept up into a stylish bun that revealed the curve of her tanned neck and the gold hoops she always wore.

"Your desserts are wonderful." Rosie lifted another bite of Sarah's dessert to her lips, eyes closing a moment as she tasted, then a broad smile broke across her face. "Did you really make these yourself, from your own recipe?"

"Yes, ma'am." Sarah nodded. When she was younger, she stayed in the kitchen as much as possible. Her recipe experiments didn't change her situation, but they kept her away from the ever-present drama of her childhood.

Rosie examined the bite thoughtfully, her expression softening. "This is perfect. Do you have other recipes like this?"

"Yes. Besides desserts, I also have main courses." Sarah handed over her recipe book.

Rosie's grin broadened as she flipped through Sarah's notes. "Step into my office. Let's talk."

As Sarah followed, she felt the weight of the staff's curious stares. The restaurant kitchen was alive with the sound of vegetables being chopped, the sizzle of meat and vegetables, and the frenetic buzz of cooks racing to prepare for the lunch rush.

Rosie closed the door, then settled into her chair, gesturing to the seat across from her desk. "You're a good waitress. Customers rave about you. Is that what you want as a career?"

"I'm not sure." Sarah perched on the edge of the chair, the soft upholstery pressing against her legs.

"I've noticed you come in early, and when you don't have a customer to wait on, you help with food preparation." Rosie tilted her head, a gentle smile easing the tension. "Why haven't you pursued becoming a chef?"

"I don't have professional training. I've worked in a few restaurant kitchens and enjoy experimenting with food."

Rosie flipped back through the recipe book. "What you have is beyond someone experimenting. These are difficult and advanced recipes. Are you sure someone hasn't trained you?"

Sarah pushed a stray hair behind her ear. "Well, when I was a teenager, my mom dated a chef at a restaurant in Dallas, and he let me help in the kitchen for a few years."

"A few years? Who was the chef?"

As soon as Sarah said the name, Rosie's eyes went wide. "What! Oh, my goodness, he's amazing and works at one of the finest restaurants in the country. Plus, he's appeared on cooking contests as a contestant and judge."

Sarah knew he was good, but didn't realize how much. "Because of his relationship with my mom, I was permitted to work in the kitchen as a helper. He was always nice to me, and as he prepared each dish, he'd explain what he was doing and why."

A dazed expression on her face, Rosie sat back in her chair. "Now I understand why your recipes are so advanced. You basically trained under one of the best."

"I don't know if I'd call it training," Sarah said with a slight shrug. "He let me come in after school during the week and on weekends to work beside him. I also worked in other restaurant kitchens over the years."

"Looking at your recipe book, I can tell. Never discount what you learned. Do you know how many people would love to work with him?" Rosie sat for a moment, then her expression turned curious. "Why wasn't that included on your resume? You only mentioned your employment at those places, not any kitchen experience."

Sarah sat on her hands to keep from wringing them. "I just wasn't sure anyone would want to know." At one point, she'd been more confident in her skills, but that was before her ex-boyfriend sabotaged her hopes and dreams.

"Give me a few minutes." Taking Sarah's recipe book with her, Rosie disappeared out the office door.

Sarah hugged her arms against herself, as if trying to hold herself together. What was she thinking, hoping for a position other than a waitress? She'd assisted cooks and chefs in other restaurant kitchens, but she wasn't someone with legitimate culinary skills.

Cooking for her mom and many boyfriends, and now for her aunt and uncle and their writing and book clubs, felt a world away from the demanding, frantic-paced life of a chef.

Maybe Rosie would let her help in the kitchen, and someday she could save up enough money to attend culinary school. Sarah glanced at the wall clock. It seemed like Rosie had been gone forever. Maybe she was trying to come up with a nice way to tell them they didn't need her anywhere but as a waitress.

Sarah sighed. She could make a living like that, and it was an honorable profession, but working in the kitchen made her feel alive.

Rosie returned, sat at her desk, and leaned forward. "My daughter, Juanita, who just had the baby, wants to cut back her days to only working part-time, so we need help in the dessert area."

Sarah grinned. "I'd be glad to help." She loved working with dough and pastries.

"Good. I've noticed how you come in early to help in the kitchen before your server duties and how skilled you are at those tasks. Chef Thomas called your mentor in Texas. Turns out they are friends from when they were starting in the industry. And you, Sarah, come highly recommended."

Sarah sucked in a breath. She couldn't believe her ears. The two chefs had decades of experience.

Rosie leaned forward, her eyes sparkling. "So, Thomas, after talking to his friend, looking at your recipe book, eating the samples you brought, said he would be thrilled to have you as his assistant." Rosie's smile widened. "Therefore, I'd like to offer you a job in the kitchen. Provided you agree, your earnings will be changed to compensate for the missing tips, and in accordance with your new position."

The words hit Sarah like a burst of sunlight. "Really? Just like that? Don't I need to work a few weeks, months, or years before you trust me?"

Rosie studied her. "Thomas and I have been watching you since you first started here. You are a wonderful server, but your kitchen skills are even more incredible. We could tell you had more to offer."

Sarah's cheeks heated. "I just wanted to help."

"Good. You are a team player and well-liked by all the staff. I know you'll do great."

Sarah blinked back happy tears. "Wow, thank you so much."

Rosie stood and offered her hand. "Welcome to the kitchen team, Assistant Chef Sarah."

Peter studied the whiteboard filled with diagrams of neural networks, equations, flowcharts, and brainstorming notes, then plopped into his chair and glanced over at Quint. "How many support tickets did you say we had?"

"In just the past seven days? Three hundred eighty-seven internal emails and support tickets," Quint groaned, rubbing his temples. "Wrestling the AI model into submission is definitely a full-time job."

Peter scrolled through his computer screen, reading the tickets and emails. The name SAUS was a play on the company owner's last name, Elijah Sausage. The original team, in a moment of wisdom, vetoed calling it SAUSAGE. After all, nobody wanted an AI that spent its days fantasizing about bratwurst or worse, demanding to be paired with mustard and pickles.

At this stage, their primary mission was to invent new training data and instructions. Which meant Peter's job essentially entailed babysitting SAUS, so it didn't start giving people tech advice like, "pour hot water on your keyboard if your monitor freezes." Their daily interactions with the model were equal parts comedic and maddening.

Quint ran his hands through his hair. "SAUS is getting way too saucy for my taste."

Peter snorted. "Job security, I guess. As long as SAUS keeps flinging out questionable answers, we'll have a reason to show up and get those hefty paychecks."

Quint reclined back in his chair. "Did you ever think back

in college that we'd be living in Garden Valley and teaching an AI not to tell people to microwave their smartphones?"

Peter shook his head. "Nope. Dream job unlocked, though."

"It's wild. I just put down money on a house in that new neighborhood. It's way too big, but maybe someday I'll fill it up." He flashed a picture of the real estate listing on his phone.

"Looks nice," Peter said. "Planning to adopt a family or a herd of robots?"

"Neither," Quint sighed. "I'm not even dating. Maybe I'll ask SAUS to set me up. Can't do worse than my last three attempts."

Peter tried not to laugh. Quintavius Sing, the AI prodigy who could debug machine learning models in his sleep, went into full system crash mode around women.

With Quint's half-Asian, half-Italian genes and blue-gray eyes, he probably had a secret fan club. Unfortunately, his pickup lines had all the charm of a software license agreement. "When you meet a woman you're interested in, you could say you design robots for a living," Peter offered. "Or just stick with machine learning engineer."

"Tried that," Quint said. 'The only response I got on a dating site was a blinking cursor."

"Do you even have a dating profile?" Peter asked.

"I deleted it after I realized that 'Emily, 24, loves hiking and poetry' was actually a chatbot hustling Bitcoin."

Peter laughed. "You fell for an AI?"

Quint's neck flamed red. "Maybe," he muttered.

"Next time, have SAUS vet your matches. He'd know if they were real or just a cleverly disguised spam bot."

"I think I'll retire from online dating and focus on my after-hours graphic design. At least that software is happy to keep me company."

"All work and no play makes Quint a dull techie. Or, you

know, a rich one with way too much square footage."

Quint smirked. "Says the man who bought a cabin so big, the Wi-Fi signal gets lost halfway to the fridge. You planning on turning mountain hermit?"

Peter put on his best sage-like expression. "I'm just settling in. A girlfriend would only complicate things. Besides, my last beard attempt looked like a mangy squirrel had a nervous breakdown on my face. Nope. Hermit life is not in my skill set."

"Excuse me," a sweet female voice said.

Peter and Quint spun around in their chairs in perfect sync as though they had practiced.

Behind them stood a petite, striking brunette, gripping a file folder.

"I was told to give you this." She handed the document to Quint, her eyes focused on him.

Stumbling out of his chair, Quint's chest rose and fell with each shaky breath, betraying how anxious he felt in the woman's presence. His neck flushed a deep shade of red as he accepted the file, his gaze fixed on her with wide, uncertain eyes.

As the two stood frozen with love-sick puppy dog eyes, Peter fought back a chuckle.

"I'm Amy," she finally said.

"Quint," his voice cracked like a teenager. He stared at her for an unusually long time, as if searching for the right words or simply overwhelmed by her presence. He audibly gulped, his mouth opening and closing like a fish out of water, struggling to form words. "Would you like to," he swallowed, "go to lunch?"

Peter almost fell out of his chair. His buddy had gone from zero to sixty on the bravery scale around women.

Amy's smile was timid as she gazed at Quint. "I think I'd like that very much." She took a pen from his desk, wrote her number on a scrap of paper, and handed it to him. "Call me when you're ready to go."

Quint stood still, his gaze tracking her every move. When she was out of sight, he let out a nervous chuckle as he clutched the number to his chest. "Did you see that? Was it real? Did that actually happen?"

Peter burst out laughing, shooting his computer a suspicious glare. "I can't believe you did that. Maybe SAUS heard us talking and sent you a girlfriend. AI dates for the relationship impaired."

"I love AI!" Quint punched the air. Then his face blanched, and he turned a wide-eyed gaze to Peter. "She wasn't an AI robot, was she?"

"No, I'm pretty confident she was real. Besides that, she was wearing a company badge, so Human Resources had to have vetted her."

A lopsided, goofy grin on his face, Quint collapsed in his chair. "I have a date with a real woman."

Peter chuckled as he got back to work. He would pay good money to watch that interaction.

As for him, today after work, he'd swing into Shaffer's Outfitters and pick up a new rod and reel to take advantage of his very own pond stocked with bass, bream, and catfish.

Women would have to wait; fish were calling his name.

Chapter 3

Even though she'd barely slept a wink, Sarah was so excited that she'd come in early to work. She stood shoulder-to-shoulder with Rosie's daughter, Juanita, at the gleaming stainless steel worktable as they worked to craft Sarah's recipe.

All around them, the kitchen was a hive of activity as the staff rushed about before the lunch crowd arrived.

Rosie had already crowned Sarah's baking creation "Sopapilla cinnamon churro bites," but the staff couldn't resist tossing in their own ridiculous ideas.

"We could call them Churropilla bites or Cinnachurropilla," offered Chef Thomas.

Another snorted. "Cinnachurropilla? Sounds like a cinnamon-dusted chihuahua."

"Sopacinnachurro!" hollered a server from the far end.

Juanita, who looked like a younger version of her mother with a cascade of long dark hair and sparkling brown eyes, shot a sly smile at Sarah. "Picture someone trying to order that with a straight face."

Sarah grinned, her hands deep in dough. "Those names would be tough to pronounce. Thanks for helping me scale up the recipe. Lately, I only cook for a few people, not half the town."

"No biggie. Growing up in a family restaurant, I could multiply recipe measurements in my sleep."

Sarah kept her voice low. "Are you sure you're okay with me helping with desserts and being an assistant chef?"

"Are you kidding?" Juanita grinned. "I've been praying for a baby forever, and now that I've got one, the last thing I want is to swap baby loving for dessert trays. We're thrilled God brought you to us."

Sarah managed a polite smile. Her journey to Garden Valley and Rosie's Restaurant was less a divine destiny and more the result of her ex-boyfriend being a jerk and her mom speeding off to California on the back of a Harley.

In her mom's world, Sarah would always be second place. Even her dad had nothing to do with her. Thank goodness Dot and Ulysses had opened their home and given her a safe place to live.

Juanita cut the dough and laid it out on a tray. "Why didn't you apply to work in the kitchen instead of as a server?"

"There weren't any openings when I moved to town, plus I thought I'd play it safe."

"After seeing your recipe book and hearing what Mom and Thomas said, it's clear you have the skills to be a chef."

A flicker of hope cautiously peeked out of Sarah's heart. She loved working in kitchens, with their hurried, lively pace, creating mouthwatering entrées or desserts for their clients.

A disturbing memory clawed its way back into her thoughts. Her ex-boyfriend's malicious actions had ruined her career and shattered her confidence.

Sarah dusted the flour off her hands and shooed away the gloomy memory. She had a new opportunity and needed to leave the rest behind.

Garden Valley looked like the place she could finally settle.

Peter tore his eyes from the endless parade of code on his

monitor and shot a look at Quint, who was positively glowing with post-date giddiness. "I'm still in shock. You've had lunch and then dinner with Amy, and you said you managed to string words together without breaking into awkward statistics."

Quint's goofy grin hadn't left his face since yesterday. "It was unbelievable. Honestly, we talked like we were friends from another life. And guess what? We're going out again tonight."

"Okay, Romeo, spill. What could you possibly talk about for two entire meals?"

Quint counted on his fingers. "We kicked things off with work, then college stories, family escapades, hometowns, and, believe it or not, we waded right into politics and religion."

Peter's eyebrows shot up so fast it was a wonder they didn't lodge in his hairline. "You went there? And you're both still alive? No flying forks or sudden dessert-face collisions?"

"Not a scratch. Turns out we agree on most subjects. And when we disagreed, we just hashed it out like debate club nerds without tears or dramatic exits."

Peter eyed him suspiciously. "You sure she isn't some AI prototype made exactly for you?"

Quint sipped his coffee with exaggerated dignity. "I'm hoping she's God-created, not lab-generated."

"Probably a safer bet than dating a chatbot. Speaking of which, does Amy even like AI?"

Quint leaned in. "She's, uh, not exactly a fan," he whispered, glancing around as if the computers might be spying.

"Should we worry SAUS will take offense?"

"Shhh," Quint hissed, his eyes darting to his computer screen. "Don't say the name out loud. SAUS is always listening."

Peter's voice dropped to a mock ominous whisper. "You realize we're teaching SAUS everything it knows, right? If it's jealous, it's your fault."

Quint set his mug down with a thud. "SAUS is learning fast. I swear it's got a mean streak. This morning, it sent me a message about the hazards of dating humans."

Peter's jaw dropped. "Get out. It did not."

"Suit yourself, but call SAUS an 'it' one more time and watch your inbox fill with passive-aggressive emojis."

"You're a walking sci-fi cliché," Peter said, shaking his head. "Hopefully, having conversations with real people might save you from going full robot."

Quint's phone buzzed. He studied his cellphone and went so pale that Peter considered checking for a pulse. "It's Amy. Her computer just crashed." Quint's eyes narrowed at Peter. "I told you. SAUS is jealous, and now it's sabotaging her! This is how the robot apocalypse starts." He shot out of his chair and bolted from the room.

Left alone, a chill climbing his spine, Peter stared at his own monitor. He typed: "You're not causing any trouble, are you, SAUS?"

"Who, me?" the reply flashed on his screen.

Every cheesy sci-fi movie Peter ever watched flickered through his mind about rogue computers and world domination.

Laughter erupted from the far side of the office.

Harrison Miller, his bodybuilder-looking coworker, grinning like he'd just won the office prank Olympics, walked toward him. "Edwards, you and Sing are way too easy. You both really thought SAUS was jealous and causing trouble?" He sauntered away, still chuckling.

Slumped in his chair, Peter stared at his screen. He should've known better. Working with AI came with its own problems, especially when factoring in pranksters like Harrison, who messed with the computer code.

Peter studied his computer screen. They were only

beginning to understand the rewards and risks involved with artificial intelligence.

Chapter 4

Nine thirty at night, and Garden Valley looked peaceful and still as Sarah left the restaurant. Only Rosie's and the General Store were open until nine. Most businesses closed their doors at seven.

Sarah drove her car down the winding driveway to her aunt and uncle's spacious, light-gray colonial home. The well-lit property sat on a large, well-manicured green lawn with foundation shrubs, a weeping Cherry, and mature trees in the back, reminding Sarah of a park.

Throughout her childhood, she'd been blessed to visit their home at various times when Heather was away with whoever she was dating.

Eager to share about her day, Sarah parked her car on the concrete pad next to the two-car garage and hurried through the sunporch. She stepped into the family room, which had a beautiful stone fireplace and built-in bookcases brimming with books and decorative items.

Five children had been raised here, and Sarah could still imagine the laughter of playing hide and seek with her cousins in the big house. All of them now lived in various parts of the country with their own families and would visit on holidays and for other family functions.

Searching through the house, Sarah stopped in her aunt and uncle's office. Bookshelves lined the walls, and two empty desks faced the large picture window overlooking the illuminated backyard. She kept looking, finally spotting Dot sitting on the back patio. Sarah hurried outside. "What are you doing out here?"

"I'm enjoying the beautiful night. How was your day?" Dot asked.

"It was great." Sarah sat next to her aunt in their comfortable, padded chair. "I worked with Juanita on the desserts and then Chef Thomas on the entrees. It was awesome. The day flew by." She took off her shoes and rubbed her sore feet. "My desserts were a big hit, and Chef Thomas loved my shrimp recipe. Rosie's going to add it to the menu next week."

"I'm so glad everything worked out well. I always knew you would be a chef. You had forgotten your talents."

"Yeah, I guess I had." Sarah gazed up at the night sky, taking in the vast, dark expanse. She was only a speck in the cosmos, not someone the world would notice.

"Don't let anyone do that to you again. Take away your confidence." Dot laid her hand on Sarah's arm. "God gifted you with unique talents, and no one can take that away."

"My old boyfriend sure did try." At that thought, the all-too-familiar ache twisted in Sarah's chest.

"He was jealous of your skills and wanted to bring you down to his level."

"He just about finished me."

"No, he didn't finish you. He just pushed you down for a while. Like a Phoenix rising from the ashes, you are flying free now."

The evening song of crickets filled the air, and the stars twinkled, as if inviting Sarah to feel hopeful again.

"Speaking of birds," Dot said. "This morning, a small bird perched on a branch would look around and then open its little beak to the sky and chirp a tune. Again and again, the bird would stop, turn its beak to the sky, and deliver a song with the passion of an opera singer." Dot gazed upward in thought before she looked again at Sarah. "Don't you think that bird was singing praises? We have so much to be thankful for with our loving God."

Sarah gave a polite nod. She believed in God, but if He was loving, why had she been placed with her mother? Ready for a subject change, Sarah glanced at Dot. "Where's Uncle Ulysses?"

"He's at his brother's house with their buddies. It's their night to sit around and solve the world's problems. Between discussions of sports, politics, and childhood memories, they enjoy one another's company."

"I can only imagine. So, how's your story coming?"

"We're on chapter twenty, and our character is about to solve the mystery."

"I don't know how you write novels."

"Prayer, persistence, a touch of humor, and hope that the characters will behave and do what we want them to do."

Sarah chuckled. "It tickles me you can have suspense books and make them fun."

"Life is filled with difficulties. Our readers can experience stories that show people can go through hardship and still have hope and overcome their obstacles."

"I'd like to write more hope into my story," Sarah murmured.

"Your story has changed for the better, don't you think? You're now a chef at the finest Mexican Restaurant this side of Tennessee, and you live with world-famous novelists." Dot nudged Sarah with her shoulder. "Or at least our version of world-famous."

"You sure you don't mind me staying here? Now that I've gotten a raise, I could get my own place."

Dot stared at her with a horrified expression. "Don't you

dare leave. We have plenty of space, and knowing you're upstairs makes us and the house happy again."

Sarah loved her upstairs bedroom, complete with a private bathroom, and the extra room she used for a sitting area with her TV. "Only if you're sure."

"Of course, we're sure," Dot said. "And if you want to decorate your rooms, feel free to make them your own."

Sarah stared at her aunt. "Really?"

"Of course. You're part of our family. Just pretend it's your own apartment. That's part of the deal in our house. The last kid in the nest gets to decorate their space. Next time you're off work and want to go furniture shopping, I'd love to join you."

"Shopping?" The thought made Sarah's heart jump. She hadn't been able to decorate her own room. *Ever*. Not with all the moving around they did when she was younger. Even when she had her own apartment, she was afraid to spend money because her mom would often show up, acting destitute and begging for a handout.

Dot patted Sarah's arm, bringing her back to the present. "Want to join me tomorrow morning at the General Store to pick up a few supplies? Since you'll be occupied in the kitchen at the restaurant, I'll need your easy recipe ideas. Writing is easy. Preparing meals has never been my specialty.

"When you finally get a day off," Dot continued, "we should go to the furniture stores and find something you like. You need a new loveseat in your TV room, and if you want a new bedroom suite, we'd love to help you get whatever you want."

"You don't need to do that."

"I know. But it's fun to shop for those I love."

Sarah's lip trembled. "Aww, thank you. I love you, too."

"Heather birthed you," Dot said as she stood and pulled Sarah to her feet and gave her a big hug, "but you are the daughter of my heart."

Sarah, nestled in her aunt's embrace, watched a shooting star streak across the twilight sky.

A tender hope settled in Sarah's heart. Maybe things had finally changed for the better.

Peter sat on his back deck, staring at the stars above. After fishing from his spring-fed pond and then preparing and cooking his meal, he felt like a real pioneer.

Then again, he couldn't imagine clearing land, building a cabin, and having to forage for food. But it was nice to step away from life's busyness and enjoy nature.

He'd always lived in close-knit neighborhoods or busy apartments. Far from any other houses, the silence of his new, remote home was refreshing.

Peter leaned back and closed his eyes. His grandad once owned five acres of land in the hills of Kentucky that he used as a quiet getaway from the fast-paced business world. He told Peter that sometimes people needed to spend time outside to let their souls catch up after the rush and hurry of life.

A rustling sound in the woods to Peter's right drew his attention. He rose to his feet, straining his eyes in the dim light to identify the shape, but the darkness made it impossible.

The rustling came again, followed by a low growl as though something was getting ready to pounce.

Backing away, Peter hurried inside and locked his door. So much for his manly pioneer thoughts. Tomorrow, he'd invest in a high-powered flashlight and a pellet pistol or something more substantial.

Maybe he should have given purchasing an isolated

property like this a lot more thought.

Chapter 5

Garden Valley closed its doors early but sprang to life even earlier. By eight in the morning, the town hummed with activity. Sarah made her second pass around the Courthouse Square.

She cruised past a charming array of shops, boutiques, antique stores, Shaffer's Outfitters, and cozy restaurants, finally easing into a parking spot near the General Store.

Locking her car door, she hurried to where Dot waited. Walking in together, they entered the historic two-story building. The door's ancient bell jingled an eager welcome.

Her aunt paused, her eyes scanning the store. "Some of my earliest happy memories are of this place."

Sarah nodded. She loved coming here. The store itself was a living time capsule, with shelves filled with an eclectic mix of groceries, hardware, and souvenirs, alongside homemade items from local artisans and even an old-fashioned soda fountain.

"Dot! Good to see you." Oswald Chambers, the rotund, silver-haired store manager, hustled toward them.

"Oswald, good to see you, too." Dot bumped fists with him. "Got any juicy stories for me? I need something for my next novel."

"Not really." He shrugged, his lips twitching with the beginnings of a grin. "Just your run-of-the-mill stuff. Nothing novel-worthy, unless you count the great orange avalanche in the produce section. Beatrice Finklebine decided to liberate an orange from the very bottom of the pyramid, and whoosh! Oranges tumbled everywhere, bouncing off shelves and rolling under carts. The whole place smelled like citrus chaos. You should've seen the customers dodging flying fruit like it was dodgeball night at the senior center."

Dot laughed. "I'll have to try to incorporate that into a novel sometime. My hero could distract the bad guy with a fruit avalanche."

Oswald beamed. "I can't wait to read that one."

"Dot, you better come see me!" Melba Marshall, the silver-haired lady, called from behind the soda fountain.

Her aunt winked at Sarah. We'd best get caught up on the gossip."

They walked to the round, red-cushioned stools and took a seat.

"Have you heard the latest?" Melba lowered her voice to a whisper. "The land and cabin next to me were sold to some young guy who works at SAU Tech. I swear, how someone that young can afford a nice cabin and land like that is beyond me. That property needs a family, real folks to love it."

"Maybe he's a nice young man," Dot said.

Melba huffed. "He's probably a whipper-snapper who will turn the land into a four-wheeler, motorcycle race course."

Dot arched an eyebrow. "Still thinking the best about people, are you?"

Melba's lips pressed so tightly they almost vanished. Then her shoulders sagged. "Fine. I'll give the boy a chance. Might even drop by this weekend with a homemade pie and check him out." Her eyes slid to Sarah, glinting with mischief. "Maybe you could join me and see if he's someone interesting."

Sarah held up her hands. "No, thank you. I am not looking for a man." That's the last thing she needed right now.

"No worries. I'll be happy to report back if I find the young man suitable for further investigation."

"Did someone say investigation?" A young woman with her brown hair pulled up into a messy but attractive bun walked toward them, her sandals slapping out a rhythm on the old wooden floors.

"Georgia Shaffer Briscoe, you come for your usual root beer float?" Melba asked, snatching up a soda glass with grace.

"You know it." Georgia perched on a stool, turning to beam at Dot and Sarah. "Hi, Ms. Dot. This must be your niece." Her smiling gaze swept over Sarah's face." I've seen you at Rosie's."

Sarah grinned. "And you're the salsa lover."

"You betcha. Root beer floats in the mornings, salsa as much as possible during the week make for a happy woman."

"Georgia's our town's private eye, you know," Dot said. "She and our local policewoman, Tonya, have been an excellent resource for our novels."

Georgia snorted a laugh. "You have asked some *very* interesting questions."

"We try to use you girls so we don't get placed on an FBI watch list for asking how to murder people," Dot said with a cheeky grin. "The CIA once turned up on the doorstep of one of our writer friends, looking very official and ready to uncover some international intrigue. All they discovered was a novelist with a wild imagination and a suspiciously enormous collection of coffee mugs."

"I can understand that happening after reading your novels," Georgia said. "It's like I open the first page and you grab me by the throat and won't let me go until the end."

Dot beamed. "That makes it all worthwhile."

Mabel finished making the float for Georgia and then turned to Sarah. "I hear you're quite the whiz in Rosie's kitchen. Isn't it unusual for someone to possess skills in so many areas?"

Sarah shrugged. "I guess I never thought about it. Whatever

needs to be done, I want to do, plus cooking and baking have always been enjoyable."

"She should be titled a master chef," Dot said proudly.

Georgia took a sip of her root beer float and glanced at Sarah. "I'm impressed. I cook to survive, not for enjoyment. Cookbooks are like a foreign language. Thank goodness Clint is agreeable to anything other than liver."

"I'm with Clint on that one." Dot chuckled. "So, are you enjoying married life?"

Georgia's expression turned dreamy. "It's wonderful."

Sarah turned away, pressing a hand to her chest as she stared at the floor. She couldn't imagine a happy marriage, not for herself. She leaned in close to her aunt and kept her voice low. "I'll get a cart and grab your things."

Dot's eyes softened in understanding as she patted Sarah's arm. "Thank you, sweet thing."

List in hand, Sarah hurried off, the cart's wheels clattering over the wood floor. She didn't have time for a man, her past, or anything other than decorating her rooms upstairs and her new position at the restaurant. Today, she was showing Chef Thomas another one of her recipes.

Maybe all those years working in various kitchens and experimenting with food had finally paid off. She found it amazing that Rosie trusted her, and Chef Thomas was so open to new ideas. Maybe God hadn't forgotten her after all.

Peter shuffled out of the team sync, the bitter aftertaste of coffee still clinging to his tongue. The fluorescent lights of the office buzzed overhead like anxious bees as he sat in his chair and mentally reviewed his to-do list: first, inspect the overnight model training run for any error rate explosions; second, whip up a Python script to wring the quirky features out of the user logs. Programming SAUS was challenging enough without the quirks stemming from logical misinterpretations of data or overly literal responses to commands.

Quint sat next to him. "SAUS is going to flip when he sees what GNNs can do for his pathing. We've got to try it."

Peter cracked a wry smile. "Sounds good. Our AI deserves the royal treatment."

"By the way, turns out the mobile app data is a circus compared to desktop. I spent two hours last night wrangling a normalization script."

"Didn't you have a date with Amy?"

"I did. We finished by ten, so I was back home serenaded by the gentle hum of the CPU until midnight."

Peter shook his head. "I don't know how you do it. I'm hard-wired for early shutdown. Even in college, I was allergic to late nights."

"I remember," Quint said with a sigh. "You were the only one at the dorm who thought bedtime was at nine."

"Kept me away from the wild parties and preserved my brain cells. The only hangover I want is from too much data, not alcohol."

"SAUS would definitely approve. Our AI overlord loves a responsible programmer."

"True," Peter shot a glance at his computer screen. "Any more cryptic messages from our resident digital phantom?"

Quint rolled his chair closer, nearly colliding with a tangle of power cords. "Not since we unmasked Harrison Miller as the culprit. And Amy's computer meltdown? Just a garden-variety tech glitch, no AI drama, just loose cables and a dusty fan."

"Maybe we should unleash SAUS on Miller," Peter said. "I

bet our AI could compose some spectacularly unnerving emails. Or maybe just swap his desktop icons with pictures of rubber ducks."

Quint rubbed his hands together. "Revenge, AI-style. The future is now, my friend."

Chapter 6

Trying not to drool, **P**eter stared at Rosie's menu. Judging from the extensive list of options, he should have visited sooner. And with his stomach rumbling in full force, he shouldn't have waited until one o'clock to eat lunch.

Quint jabbed a finger at the menu insert, eyes gleaming. "Check out their new additions. Ever heard of a Sopapilla cinnamon churro bite?"

Peter grinned, "Nope, but my taste buds are planning a full-scale invasion as soon as I pick my entrée."

"Chicken fajitas for me."

"Shrimp Veracruz is calling my name."

After placing their order, Peter took in the restaurant's atmosphere. The walls splashed with colors brighter than a code editor in dark mode, while Mexican music bounced from the speakers, energetic but not too loud.

The server delivered the chips and salsa along with their water.

"Was Amy busy for lunch?" Peter asked Quint.

"Yeah, she's clocking overtime, some monster project. We'll catch up later tonight."

"I'm impressed you still have fresh topics to discuss."

Quint snorted. "Come on, I've dated before. You, on the other hand, need to debug your social life."

"Maybe." Peter took a chip, nearly dropping it in his lap. "Still kind of gun-shy after that last one."

Quint gazed at Peter. "I never got why you dated her in the

first place."

Peter winced, remembering the wasted hours. "Her beauty was striking, but her interior lacked the same brilliance. My brain was clearly suffering a meltdown into stupidity."

Quint munched on a chip. "Too bad people don't come with warning labels. SAUS would probably love to generate those for you."

"No thanks. I don't need an AI audit of my life."

"I bet SAUS would call you a hard-working guy, guarding his heart in the wilds of life."

"Not the worst diagnosis." Peter shrugged. "I thought living on acreage would be peaceful. Which it is, except when the nighttime turns into a mystery podcast."

Quint flipped a chip at him. "You afraid of the silence, city boy?"

Peter grabbed and ate the morsel. "It's not the quiet that gets me. It's the random thumps and growls outside. Last night, I swear a bear was auditioning for a horror movie by my back deck."

"This area's got plenty of bears. They haven't recently made news headlines, but unless you're volunteering to be the main course, I'd steer clear of anything that massive with claws," Quint said with a shudder.

"When I was a kid," Quint continued," my family visited the Smoky Mountain State Park. I kid you not, people saw bears and thought since they were park animals, they must be friendly cartoon characters. People would leap out of their cars and dash over for selfies, like the bears were about to sign autographs. Total madness."

Peter snorted. "Yeah, no. My bucket list doesn't include getting hugged by anything that could turn me into a snack pack. I need a dog with a big, loud bark that screams 'Wildlife, you shall not pass!'"

"But then you'd need to be home more, unless you give the dog remote access privileges."

Peter dipped a chip into the salsa. "I wouldn't chain it outside. But you're right. My long hours wouldn't be fair to any animal."

"Robot canine?" Quint suggested, raising his eyebrows.

"No way. I spend all day with AI. The last thing I want at home is a canine coded in Java. Security lights and cameras will have to do."

Why had he bought that land and cabin? He wasn't even that much of an outdoor guy. The countless westerns he'd watched with his Grandad growing up must have had more influence on him than he thought.

Peter dipped his chip, then closed his eyes, enjoying the flavorful, spicy salsa. He should have prayed and thought more before the purchase. The property was beautiful, but he didn't need anything that big, and he missed having close neighbors.

Maybe he should sell and find something else. But he'd lose money on that deal, and where would he live if he did? It wasn't like his place would have gone up in price yet.

Their meals arrived with fajitas hissing and shrimp glistening.

Peter watched the server walk back to the kitchen. Through the swinging doors, he caught a glimpse of the most stunning woman he'd seen in ages.

He quickly redirected his gaze to his sizzling plate, reminding himself that with women, he needed to remember substance over style, character over beauty.

Of course, a little attraction in the female algorithm wouldn't hurt, but he'd keep focused on work and not be tempted by the fairer sex.

Peter took a big bite of his food and groaned with pleasure at the explosion of flavors. He would definitely come back to this restaurant.

An older white-haired gentleman at the next table sighed, "The property we found is perfect, but the access goes through someone else's land."

"We can ask the Realtor to contact them and see if they would give us permission," the younger man next to the older gentleman said. "If not, we'll find something. Our veterans deserve a place to get away for a while to help with their mental and physical healing."

"I agree. We have a great counseling team in place to help the vets who are struggling with post-traumatic stress. God will provide what we need. We'll keep praying," the older man said, his voice thick with emotion. "I honestly believe God brought us here, so we'll trust that He will direct us."

Peter's food stuck in his throat. His Grandad had been a veteran who proudly served his country. Was the conversation next to him a mere coincidence or something else?

His cabin was backed by forty acres, accessible only by going through his land. Were they talking about his place? If they were, maybe he could speak to his realtor about how to grant someone access.

While Quint chatted away about SAUS and what they would work on later, Peter couldn't help wondering if he was to do more than provide a way for someone to access the land behind him. His parents and family had always been generous in helping others. What if he was supposed to donate or sell some of his property to the vet ministry?

Peter took a big swig of his ice water, trying to cool and calm his thoughts. Surely, that wasn't what he needed to do. Maybe he could find out what the men were talking about and donate a few dollars.

As the men continued to discuss their mission to help the vets, Peter sent up a silent prayer for guidance, and that he wouldn't do anything he shouldn't.

After work, he'd talk to God, his parents, check his bank account, and contact his realtor.

Sarah placed the plate in the warming area for the server. Even though it was after one, the busy lunch crowd still kept the kitchen hopping.

The atmosphere buzzed with the rhythmic thumping of cleavers on cutting boards and the sizzle of marinated meats hitting the hot grill. Aromas of roasted poblanos, fresh cilantro, and smoky chipotle created an intoxicating perfume that filled the air.

Chef Thomas glanced at her, a smile tugging at his lips, visible in the crinkles around his dark-brown eyes. "Keep up the good work."

Sarah stood a little straighter as she worked at the grill next to the man who had readily accepted her, her heart thrumming with adrenaline and pride.

Servers went in and out of the kitchen while those working at the various stations stayed busy preparing appetizers, salads, and all finishing sauces. Other workers were dedicated to making and grilling fresh tortillas and other masa products. The constant chatter created an orchestrated symphony of orders called out, quick jokes exchanged, and staff encouraging one another over the roar of the vent hoods.

Sarah couldn't help but grin. She loved the rush and excitement of a team of employees working together like a well-oiled machine, creating delicious dishes for Rosie's clientele.

Some people thought it was crazy to enjoy something so stressful and high-paced, but to Sarah, it infused her bones with energy, as if she were made for this life.

The satisfaction of sending out a beautiful plate of food and seeing a customer's face light up at a perfectly prepared meal made every frantic moment worth it.

The camaraderie among the staff, the shared pride when a diner's delighted gasp drifted from the dining room, and the warmth of knowing she was part of something special.

Sarah focused on her task at the grill. She should have fought back when her ex-boyfriend sabotaged her. Instead, she'd been so hurt and surprised he would do such a terrible thing, she'd just left and walked away from a job she loved.

Then again, how could she have challenged the man who was the son's owner? She never had a chance to prove her innocence.

A terrible thought ran through her mind. Was she like Heather, who was always running away from life? Sarah shook her head. No. No way. She was *not* like her mother. Never again would she allow someone to mess with her life and her future. Not Heather and not any man. She would keep focused on her work, her aunt and uncle, and enjoy the life she'd been given.

Rosie walked toward them, her eyes shining with excitement. "I have exciting news. SAU Tech has asked us to cater a meal for the AI department. Sarah, I'd like you to join our servers and share a few words about the restaurant. I think you'd make an excellent impression."

Sarah's stomach dropped. "Me?"

Chef Thomas grinned. "I agree with Rosie. You would be an excellent choice to represent us."

"But I haven't worked here that long. Shouldn't someone

else do that? Like Chef Thomas?"

Rosie patted Sarah on the arm. "I think you're the perfect choice."

Sarah gulped. It had been years since she'd gone out with a catering team. How could she make a speech or even say a few words in front of people? She glanced back and forth between Chef Thomas and Rosie. "But what would I say?"

"Explain what we make," Chef Thomas said as he continued his cooking. "Highlight the pride we have in preparing our food. How we use only the freshest local produce and the finest meat."

Rosie grinned. "You'll be our goodwill ambassador."

Sarah's hands trembled as she twisted the edge of her apron, her breath catching in her throat. She got tongue-tied speaking to more than two people.

"From the look on your face," Rosie said with a soft laugh. "I know you're struggling. I'll send Juanita and a few others with you to help. You won't be alone. I'm not asking you to make a long speech, just give them some quick details about the restaurant and what we serve."

Sarah blew out a calming breath. She wouldn't have to talk about herself, only the restaurant and the people who had given her a second chance to do what she loved. Yes, she could definitely do that.

Couldn't she?

Chapter 7

Saturday afternoon, Peter meandered through the meadow in front of his cabin, grass brushing his jeans and wildflowers bobbing in the breeze.

The mountain backdrop stretched up like a green giant taking a nap, and for a moment, Peter breathed in the scent of pine and sun-warmed earth, as his brain finally slowed down.

He'd done all the responsible adult things, prayed, researched the vet ministry until his eyes crossed, called his parents for advice, and begged them to include him in their prayers. The more prayer coverage, the better.

Mom and Dad, seasoned Realtors with a love of spreadsheets and strong opinions, practically swooned over the nonprofit's stellar rep and their top-notch work for veterans. His parents rattled off all sorts of financial wisdom. If Peter let folks cross his land, he could get paid up front, or let them deal with the property taxes, or fix the pothole-filled road.

Peter wandered to the pond where the water was so still it looked like a mirror. And right now, it was reflecting his confused expression.

He plopped down on the grass, running through the same old worries. Letting the ministry have access through the land was a given. But what about selling the place? Give it away? Peter groaned. If he donated the entire property, folks would probably start sending him flyers for free psychiatric evaluations.

He couldn't quite figure out why he felt led to do something so wild as giving away his cabin and land. Why not just toss a few hundred bucks their way and keep his comfy life? Then again, it wasn't like he needed the cash. His salary was so hefty it practically needed its own zip code.

Peter sprawled out on the grass, watching the clouds drift by in shapes that looked somewhat like dancing cows. A memory popped up from his childhood, when he helped at the homeless shelter. As a kid, he'd wished he could do more than donate the twenty-five dollars he'd saved from mowing lawns. He remembered praying, asking God to help him be generous when he grew up.

Now he was rolling in dough, clinging to his land and money tighter than a squirrel with its last acorn. Somewhere, Scrooge was shaking his finger at him.

A sudden rumble snapped him out of his existential spiral. A red pickup, engine growling like an angry bear, roared toward him and stopped. Out hopped a silver-haired woman, ponytail swinging.

"I'm your neighbor, just over that hill," she jerked her thumb west. "Melba Marshall. Brought you something." With a flair, she presented a still-steaming apple pie, nestled in a kitchen towel.

Peter's stomach responded with a growl as he accepted the offering. "Thank you. Nice to meet you. I'm Peter Edwards."

"Nice to meet you too. I work at the General Store soda fountain. Stop in and see me sometime, and I'll make you the best float you've ever had." Melba's gaze scanned the property before turning back toward him. "What's a young guy like you doing with this much land?"

Peter rubbed his neck. "I've been asking myself the same thing."

She smirked. "Feeling a bit isolated, are we?"

"Yeah, it's peaceful, except at night when I'm having trouble deciphering sounds from the woods. Plus, I think the squirrels are judging my fashion choices." Peter pointed to his polo shirt, then to the squirrel chattering in the tree next to them.

"You're not from the mountains, are you?" Melba grinned.

"No, ma'am. Lexington, Kentucky. Suburb bred and born."

"Had a friend from there." Melba nodded thoughtfully. "Lost her back in that Covid mess—sad business. At least I know where she is now. Knowing her, she's probably organizing angels into a choir." She pointed skyward.

Peter nodded, thinking of his grandparents, grateful for their heavenly address. "Would you like to join me on the deck for a slice of pie?"

Melba's friendly smile removed ten years from her face. "That's mighty neighborly. I love what I cook, so yes. Besides, I need to make sure you don't eat the whole thing yourself."

Peter chuckled. "I appreciate that." He showed Melba through his house, stopping in the kitchen to get plates and utensils. Melba made a few generously kind remarks about his sparsely decorated home.

Once they were on the back deck, Peter served up a slice for each of them.

They polished off the dessert while Melba painted pictures with her words of bear encounters, snowstorms, and local characters who may or may not have been related to Bigfoot.

As the sun dipped, Peter's thoughts returned to his land dilemma, and he asked if she'd heard of the vet nonprofit.

Melba's face softened. "They're the real deal. Helped my nephew through PTSD. The counselors don't just toss Bible verses and tell the vet to get over it. They listen, really listen. Helped my nephew grieve and helped him find hope." Her gaze locked onto his. "Sometimes you just need someone to sit beside you while you eat pie and figure out life."

Peter turned back to face the land behind him. Perhaps his choice wasn't as difficult as it seemed. Maybe it was about releasing his grip instead of clinging to what he possessed.

"It's eleven o'clock. Shouldn't you two be in bed?" Sarah propped against the door of her aunt and uncle's office.

Ulysses didn't even glance up, his eyes glued to the screen as his fingers danced across the keyboard. Dot, meanwhile, was lost in a blizzard of papers, wielding her red pen with all the flourish of an orchestra conductor.

Without turning around, Dot held up her hand. "Just a minute, we've had a breakthrough in the story."

"Got it!" Ulysses declared, stabbing the ENTER key. He looked over and blinked, squinting at Sarah as if she'd materialized out of thin air. "When did you get home? Have you been standing there long enough to bring snacks?"

"I just got home a few minutes ago, and no, I'm sorry to say I didn't bring snacks. Did you guys even stop for meals, or are you running solely on inspiration and coffee fumes?"

Dot, clearly working through a fog of fictional worlds, stared at her husband with a bewildered expression. "Did we eat, or did we just write about eating?"

Ulysses scratched his chin. "Well, our main character had lunch at a restaurant, and I'm pretty sure we both got hungry, so that counts, right?"

Dot snapped her fingers. "Yes! Literary osmosis. We did have a meal."

Sarah rolled her eyes. "That's it. I'm prepping meals and

stashing them in your fridge."

"You don't have to do that," Ulysses said, "but if a casserole appears, we wouldn't turn it down."

Sarah shook her head. "You two are a pair. I still don't know how or why you write mystery and suspense."

"Evil exists, and we shouldn't pretend it doesn't." Dot brandished a page like a victory flag. "We've got to learn how to live and be brave in this dark world."

Ulysses nodded. "Evil shows up uninvited and leaves life in chaos. From mean kids in school to those who wreak havoc just because, well, they're evil. We write because life's basically a crime novel where hope is the best detective. Through our characters, we get to show that God hands out flashlights for those dark chapters."

"I wish life were as easy as writing a story," Sarah sighed. "I'd prefer a fairy-tale life."

Dot stood, stretching with a groan. "You do realize fairy tales usually have evil stepmothers, dragons, death, or some other terrible thing, don't you?"

"Yes, but I meant the happy-ever after part."

Ulysses chuckled. "Ah, so you want to get to those last pages before the bad stuff."

Sarah nodded. "Of course, I do."

"The most captivating stories always feature characters enduring trials, yet emerging victorious." Dot grinned. "Just like you."

"Me?"

"You've experienced so much, and now you stand before us as a young woman who is strong, resilient, and successful. Even your cooking shows you're a winner. You take random ingredients and create edible magic. When you crack eggs, just imagine someone whose life is cracked, but with God's help, ends up a soufflé instead of scrambled."

Sarah blinked a few times as she processed. Was Dot right? Sarah pretended to yawn. She was too tired to get philosophical, "It's way too late for metaphors, soufflés, or sermons. I need to get off my feet, take a hot shower, and collapse into my soft and cozy bed."

After saying goodnight, Sarah went to her room and took off her shoes. She'd never considered that she was strong, resilient, or successful.

She had a good job and was doing reasonably well, but in reality, she was nothing more than a scrambled mess in life's skillet.

Chapter 8

Sarah slid in the biscuits and slammed the oven door, then shoved her trembling hands into her back pockets.

Why couldn't she live her own life, free from the shadow of the endless demands of her mother? Heather had sabotaged and interfered with every step Sarah took toward independence. And now Heather was arriving next week, not because she cared, but because she thought Sarah's new job meant there was money to be had.

Dot entered the kitchen, waving a black cane with a pearl handle sparkling in the light. "What do you think?"

Sarah forced herself to focus. "Why do you have a cane?"

"It's for our next story." Dot twisted the handle, revealing a hidden blade. "You like?"

"Nice. I could use one of those."

"Couldn't we all?" Dot grinned, then her brow furrowed. "What's up? Something's troubling you."

"My mother."

Dot sucked in a breath. "Enough said. What's she up to this time?"

"She's coming here for a visit."

Dot gasped, then turned to the hallway. "Battle stations, Ulysses. Heather is coming!"

Ulysses sprang into the room. "No. Here?"

"Afraid so," Sarah said. "She said she's just passing through, but said she wants to come check and make sure I'm doing well."

"Right," Dot scoffed. "Heather wants money again, doesn't

she?"

"Probably." Needing support, Sarah gripped the counter.

"Don't do it," Ulysses said as he stepped closer. "You're a grown woman. You have your own life and career. You are not responsible for your mother."

Sara rubbed her eyes before a tear could escape. "Heather always quotes that Bible verse about honoring your parents."

Dot huffed. "Your mom wants nothing to do with God unless it's on her terms. She's abusive and uses you to supply her extravagant lifestyle. Perhaps honoring her is helping her stand on her own two feet."

"Honoring someone doesn't mean tolerating or enabling abuse," Ulysses said. "Number one, we are to honor God. You can honor Him and honor your mom by praying for her, forgiving her, and setting healthy boundaries. You don't owe your mom financial support. She's a grown woman who has made choices since she was young to use other people to support her. It's not about what she needs; it's about wanting you to meet her wants."

Dot nodded. "She plays the victim card with complete relish. Her excuse has always been that someone else's actions kept her from being successful, or working, or even caring for her daughter." Dot rubbed Sarah's arm. "Do you want to talk to our pastor about this? I've had many conversations with him about your mother. Not to bad-mouth her, but for Godly advice and wisdom."

Sarah crossed her arms over her chest, wishing she could hug the ache away. "I don't know. What good would that do?"

"Counseling is a blessing. It offers the opportunity to process in ways that support healing. Ask God how you can love her and stay in contact in a healthy way for both of you. Speak the truth in love even if that truth hurts." Dot wrapped her arms around Sarah. "We're here for you and will help you when she comes to visit. You are part of our family, and you are not alone."

Sarah snuggled in Dot's warm embrace.

As for God? Sarah longed for a closer relationship with them. But why hadn't He intervened to protect her from her mother's actions?

Sarah fought back the tears. How on earth could she possibly do what was right when she wasn't even sure what that meant?

Standing in the den of his cabin, Peter stared at the stack of boxes. Packing his stuff wasn't difficult because he hadn't bothered to unpack in the short time he'd lived here.

Maybe part of him knew all along this wouldn't be where he would settle. He'd paid initially for most of the property with his work bonus, and the rest came from savings. And now it belonged to the vet ministry.

His time in prayer had solidified his decision. As strange as other people might think of what he'd done, he knew it was right.

Peter crossed to the French doors and stepped outside onto the back deck. The last rays of the sun dipped behind the mountains, casting long shadows and coloring the late evening sky with streaks of orange and pink. He'd miss the beauty of the land, but knowing it would be put to good use was even better.

For now, he'd stay in an apartment, then whenever he purchased something else, he'd find a house in a neighborhood where he wouldn't be as isolated.

A scattering of stars appeared in the dusky sky. Life out

here was a beautiful mix of nature's sights, sounds, and peace. A rustling sound in the bushes near the trees sent a chill down Peter's spine.

A pair of squirrels sprinted out of the undergrowth and scrambled up a tree. Peter sighed. So much for being a brave, outdoorsy kind of guy. He was definitely not cut out for life in the country. He'd stick to computers and tech expertise.

With a quick turn, he retreated inside, closing and locking the door behind him.

Chapter 9

Lost in thought, Peter stared at his computer screen, displaying real-time training metrics. The quiet hum of server racks came from their dedicated room nearby. Ever since he made his decision and met with the nonprofit and his realtor, he'd slept like a rock.

A crumpled ball of paper bounced off his shoulder.

"What is wrong with you?" Quint fired another paper missile, this time aiming for Peter's head. "You got the Monday blues?"

Peter blinked, trying to refocus on reality. "Nah, I'm fine. Just thinking about something I did this weekend."

"Do tell." Grinning, Quint moved closer. "Women troubles? Wolf and bear problems? I'm sure SAUS would be glad to give advice."

"No thanks. I don't think AI can handle anything divinely orchestrated."

"Okay, spill," Quint said, plopping his feet up on the desk. "Did you finally turn your place into a monk's retreat?"

"No, but close. Have you ever felt led to do something other people would consider crazy?"

"Sure. I went shopping with my two sisters on Black Friday." Quint gave a dramatic shudder. "Barely made it out alive."

"Probably wasn't your smartest move, but I'm talking about doing something way off the norm." Peter wheeled his chair closer. "Something because you felt a holy nudge."

Quint's eyebrows shot up, his finger pointing skyward. "You mean from above?"

Peter nodded. "I met with a group this weekend that helps veterans. They've been eyeing the land behind my property."

"Nice," Quint said. "Sounds like they'd be good neighbors."

"True, but the only way to reach the acreage is by crossing my land." Peter kept his voice quieter. "So, I could either grant them access or do something more."

"What do you mean by more? Granting them the ability to drive through your land sounds like a win for you both."

"I felt led to go further than that." Peter took a deep breath. "I donated my cabin and acreage to their nonprofit."

Quint nearly fell out of his chair. "You did what? You just gave that to them? Why did you do that? Where are you going to live?"

"I'll figure something out. Probably an apartment."

Quint's eyes locked onto Peter's, and for a fleeting moment, he seemed to question Peter's sanity. "I'm all for donating and giving to worthy charities, but how did you come to a conclusion like that? Did you open the Bible and place your finger on a verse that said donate thy land, or pray and get a word from above, or simply lose your marbles?"

"No, nothing like that. I mean, I did pray a lot. And yes, I read the Bible, but I didn't point to a verse and claim it as my own. I got advice from my parents. And after a long time in prayer, I realized that when I was a kid, I wanted to do more to help those who needed help. And this opportunity seemed to be the answer to that prayer."

Quint tilted his head as though processing. "So, a twenty-something-year prayer delay?"

"Maybe. It just felt right." Peter rubbed his neck, feeling the tension melt away. "No, it's more than a feeling; it's a soul-deep knowing that this was the time to do more than just think about helping others."

"I'm all for being generous. But don't you think you're going too far?"

"No, I think what I did was just right." With every word he uttered regarding his choice, Peter's conviction strengthened. "The group will use the cabin as the main lodge where they can provide meals and counseling. Small cabins will be added as additional space for veterans and their wives for week-long or weekend escapes. They already have a facility in Alaska, but most vets lack the resources to make such a long journey. Tennessee is a more convenient destination for most of them."

"I'm proud of you," Quint said as he eyed him. "You'll probably be famous for your generosity."

"No," Peter shook his head. "I asked that the donation be kept private. I didn't do it to be noticed by people. God gave me the money. It's His anyway. He deserves all the credit."

He felt confident he'd done the right thing, especially when his Dad shared something Peter had never known. Turns out, his grandad not only served in the armed forces, but had returned home with unseen scars, fighting through PTSD. His grandad made it through that dark time, but not without getting help along the way. Peter now understood why his Grandad would often go to the land he'd bought to get away.

The nonprofit he'd donated his property to had offered to name the lodge after his grandad and hang a picture in the lobby. Peter felt a warm surge in his chest. His grandfather's memory would be honored in a space that would provide hope and healing to those in need.

"Hey," Quint snagged his attention. "My place has plenty of space. East wing's yours. Two bedrooms and a kitchenette with no rent. No arguments. The rooms are empty, just waiting for a guest. We've been roommates before, and you're a clean guy who can cook a mean bowl of ramen."

Peter stared at his friend, surprised at his generosity. "Thanks. I'll take you up on the offer and be glad to handle a few meals. I'm great at takeout. And I promise to keep my room clean. And I can help with the rent."

"No money needed," Quint said. "But you have to promise you won't hound me if I leave a dirty dish in the sink or my clothes on the floor."

"I don't do that."

Quint's eyes narrowed. "You drove me crazy when we were in college, always harping on my not being neat enough."

Peter sent his friend a mock glare. "Fine, but I'll have you know my sisters took great pride in making me a neater man."

"Well, you can be as neat as you want in your own space. I'm not a slob, but I don't want to be a neat-freak either. Just let me know when you're ready, and I'll help move your furniture and belongings."

"Thanks. I'll keep you posted." Peter examined his desktop and reordered the items, aiming for a less structured appearance.

A relentless thumping echoed through Sarah's half-asleep mind. With a groan, she cracked open one eyelid and cringed at the sunlight streaming through her windows. It was her precious day off, and instead of silence, her ears caught a suspicious beat rising from downstairs.

Sarah shuffled out of bed, wrapped in her robe, and shoved her feet into her fuzzy slippers. Downstairs, the air pulsed with dance music so loud she could feel the bass in her chest.

Stopping at the office, Sarah watched as Dot and Ulysses, looking like disco-ball escapees with punk-rock hops, 80s elbows, and a touch of ballroom twirls, collided in a tangled, joyous mess of dance moves.

Dot shimmied over, glittering with energy, and seized Sarah's hand. "Come on, it's dance time. We just finished our novel and sent it off. Publisher-bound, baby!"

Before Sarah could protest, she was swept into a tornado of laughter and wildly enthusiastic spins. Her relatives whirled around her, their faces alight with happiness.

Caught up in the contagious fun, Sarah launched into her best ballet steps, even throwing in a dramatic pirouette that left her slightly dizzy but thoroughly delighted with clean, good fun that tickled every inch of her soul.

The music crashed to a halt, and the three collapsed onto the carpet in a heap of giggles, panting breaths, and pounding hearts.

Sarah peeked at her aunt. "Do you guys throw dance parties every time you finish a book?"

Dot nodded. "Started fifteen years ago with the novels. We've been dancing together since the day we met. It's our secret recipe for making hard things sweet."

"We even won a dance contest," Ulysses chimed in.

"True," Dot laughed, "but it was for the worst dancers in town. We took home the trophy and a set of matching earplugs."

Ulysses puffed up. "We should add that to our website that we're Champion ballroom dancers."

"Technically, we only danced in a ballroom," Dot said. "The rest is just decorative storytelling."

"Minor detail, nothing more." Ulysses got to his feet and helped Dot up, then turned to Sarah. "You are a natural. Those ballet moves are spectacular. I can tell you're a professional."

Sarah grinned as he helped her to her feet. "I actually won a dance contest once. I was five, but I owned that classroom."

Ulysses struck a dramatic dance pose. "See? We're all champions."

Looking apologetic, Dot turned to Sarah. "Hope we didn't wake you."

"No worries." Sarah stretched her back. "I probably needed to get going." She walked to the doorway and stopped. "So, you two want me to whip up breakfast?"

"Yes!" Dot and Ulysses said at the same time.

Sarah giggled. "Alright. Shower first, then breakfast magic."

Dot cranked up the volume, sending the beat bouncing off the walls. "Dance time for happy tummies!"

With each step up the stairs, Sarah's heart swelled with gratitude. She never would have thought her chaotic, turbulent childhood would be replaced with a dream job and a home filled with love, laughter, and dancing.

The ringtone of her cell phone hurried her pace. Sarah grabbed her phone off the nightstand and stared at the caller's name — her mother.

Instantly, all the lightness and hope drained away, replaced by a heavy ache in her chest and a rush of old, familiar anxiety.

Chapter 10

Sarah attempted to tamp down her nerves as she arranged the fajita meat on the serving tray for delivery. Today was the big day to deliver the meal at SAU Tech. She still didn't understand why she'd been chosen to talk about the restaurant.

"I have faith you can do this." Rosie came next to her as though she'd read Sarah's mind. "Let your team handle the meal service while you provide some background on the restaurant."

"I don't know any of the people at the company, and Juanita and everybody else know much more than I do about the restaurant." Despite her best efforts, Sarah wasn't successful in keeping her voice from sounding whiny.

"They have been here longer, but now you're one of our chefs."

"But Jaunita's smarter, prettier, and has the restaurant bloodline coursing through her veins, and I'm a nobody."

Rosie placed her hand on Sarah's arm. "Stop that negative talk. You are a smart, beautiful, talented woman who is a highly skilled member of our team. Why all this self-doubt? You seem to have shrunk the last couple of days."

Her chest tightening, Sarah wrapped the tray in aluminum foil. "My mother is coming to visit."

"From your reaction, I take it that isn't a good thing?"

"No. Not really. It's not like you have with your family."

"I'm sorry." Rosie took Sarah's hands in hers. "I don't know what issues you and your mother may have, but te considero una de mis hijas."

Juanita nudged Sarah with her shoulder. "That means she considers you one of her daughters."

Sarah held a hand to her chest. "Aw, thank you, Rosie."

Rosie smiled. "Now, get your sweet little tail out the door and to SAU Tech and rave about our awesome restaurant."

Peter's stomach grumbled, a clear sign of hunger, since he'd had three cups of coffee this morning and not a bite to eat. He made his way into the conference room and noted the long table covered with food.

The mouthwatering aroma of Mexican cuisine wrapped around him like a warm tortilla. Peppers sizzled, cheese melted somewhere in the background, and salsa glistened in little bowls.

Barely resisting the urge to drool, he took his seat next to Quint. Peter couldn't believe the company was actually springing for a lunch this good to mark their team's recent accomplishments. If they did this every time they hit a milestone, he'd be a happy and well-fed tech man.

As he watched the servers preparing the food, he spotted the gorgeous long-haired brunette he'd seen through the kitchen doors at Rosie's.

Their SAU Tech team leader stood up, launched into the standard "Great job, keep it up" speech, and sprinkled in some motivational confetti. But Peter was deaf to all of it. His attention tunneled to the vision by the buffet. He hadn't dreamed about her yet, but if his subconscious ever took requests, he knew who'd be starring.

The woman stepped forward, or more falter-stepped forward. Her face bright red, and her voice wobbly, she thanked everyone for letting Rosie's cater. She said some other nice things about the restaurant and immediately retreated, looking like she'd rather be hiding.

He understood those feelings. Maybe they had some things in common. Peter rose to his feet and plotted a course toward her.

His coworker, Harrison, body-blocked him. "She's mine, Edwards. Step aside and let a real man take the lead."

Quint jabbed Peter in the back. "Don't let him get in your way."

Peter's feet, however, seemed to be glued to the carpet as his confidence trickled away. He felt like he was again the awkward, geeky kid from middle school, who had tripped over his own backpack and never could talk to girls.

Shaking off that unpleasant thought, Peter took a deep breath, pushed his glasses up his nose, and propelled himself to the serving line.

He took a plate and silverware, then pointed to the mountain of fajitas as his choice. The comforting warmth of grilled chicken and sautéed onions filled his nostrils and calmed his racing heart.

He gazed at the woman, now cornered by Harrison. Her beautiful, gray-eyed gaze flicked toward Peter as though silently pleading for help. If wilderness skills measured bravery, he'd probably get eaten by a squirrel, but this was his moment.

Summoning every scrap of courage and aiming skills honed from years of shooting paper balls at trash cans, Peter took his fork and, with a flick of the wrist, sent a sliver of chicken flying.

It spun through the air and landed on Harrison's shoulder with a satisfying splat.

Harrison spun around, eyes narrowed. "Did you do that?"

Peter shrugged, feigning innocence. "Sorry, it must have

slipped." Inside, he was high-fiving his inner superhero.

Harrison, muttering words that were not fit for polite company, grabbed a napkin and tried to dab away the chicken carnage as he made a hasty exit.

Peter noticed the woman grinning at him, her eyes twinkling with gratitude. Internally, he did a victory fist pump. *Yes!*

She took a tiny step toward him. "Thank you."

"You're more than welcome. I'm Peter Edwards," he said, nearly dropping his plate in excitement.

"Sarah Livingstone." She dipped her head, cheeks tinged pink.

"Thanks for bringing a great meal. And you did a nice job talking about the restaurant." He wished he could come up with something suave or debonair. But he wasn't even sure what those words meant.

"Thank you for the compliment," Sarah said in her sweet voice.

"My pleasure." Peter adjusted his glasses again, hoping he looked more like Clark Kent in Superman disguise than a geeky nerd. He gave her another smile, then finished making his way down the serving line and hurried to sit next to Quint. "Did you see that?"

Quint chuckled as he grabbed a chip and dipped it in the bowl on their table. "I'm impressed. You saved the damsel in distress."

"Her name's Sarah," Peter said with a sigh. Man, he was head over heels with someone he'd just met.

His friend jerked his thumb toward the doorway, where the unmistakable scent of vengeance mixed with roasted chicken drifted from Harrison. "Miller looks ready to pulverize you."

Peter stabbed a forkful of refried beans, shot his friend a

mischievous grin, and stage-whispered, "Totally worth it. I'll just talk to SAUS and ask the AI to install a security laser grid around my cubicle."

"Protective lasers? You should be more worried about protecting your ribs. Remember when I told you to take that self-defense class while we were in college?"

Peter rolled his eyes. "You know I didn't. I've watched at least three martial arts tutorials, though."

"Well, you're basically a ninja then. Maybe you can fend off Harrison with your deadly knowledge of YouTube."

Peter looked at Sarah, who was laughing with the other servers. Honestly, if Harrison clobbered him into next week, he figured he'd still die happy.

The smell of fajitas, the thrill of victory, and the memory of Sarah's grateful smile were all totally, absolutely worth it.

Chapter 11

Balancing the empty food trays, Sarah waited by the back door and gave a grateful nod as the server opened the heavy door for her. The hum of clattering dishes and the warmth of simmering pots greeted her as she stepped inside.

Juanita nudged Sarah's arm. "It was so sweet how that handsome guy in glasses jumped in to help save you from that flirty guy."

Sarah grinned as she set the trays down in the wash area. "He was cute, wasn't he?" His wavy dark brown hair and big brown eyes behind his glasses reminded her of Superman in disguise, like Clark Kent.

"It's a shame you didn't give him your number."

Sarah's fingers fidgeted with the edge of a tray. "Peter didn't ask."

"You remembered his name. That's a good sign. He seemed shy. He probably worked up his courage to come to your rescue. I could tell he wanted to know you better."

Sarah shrugged, a pang of insecurity twisting inside her. "I'm nothing special."

Compassion shone in Juanita's eyes. "We've got to get you some confidence."

The rush of footsteps announced Rosie's arrival. She bounced toward them. "How did it go?"

"Sarah did great," Juanita said. "And the Tech group devoured the food. Tons of compliments and promises to visit the restaurant."

Rosie's face lit with pride. "I knew it would go well. The manager already contacted me, letting me know the team loved every bite and enjoyed what you shared."

"Thank you." A surge of satisfaction warmed Sarah's chest. "Honestly, I didn't do that great, but the food was outstanding. Kudos to Chef Thomas!" she called across the kitchen.

Caught in the haze of smoke and sizzling meat, Chef Thomas grinned. "Don't forget you helped. Kudos right back to you."

A sudden, urgent voice cut through the kitchen bustle. "Ma'am, wait!"

Sarah's mother swept into the kitchen like a whirlwind. Heather's bottle-blonde hair shimmered under the fluorescent lights, catching every eye. As usual, she was dressed in skin-tight jeans and a top with a plunging neckline that highlighted her artificially enhanced bust.

Her mother's blue-contacted gaze searched the room until she spotted Sarah. "There she is!" Heather rushed over and cupped Sarah's cheeks with her manicured fingers. Her fancy, expensive rings glittered, likely gifts from another wealthy man she was dating. "My darling daughter."

Embarrassment prickled along Sarah's skin as she fought the urge to shrink away. Heather only used the term "darling" when she was putting on a show of being a good mother.

"So this is where my baby works." Heather's hips swung as she strutted toward the grill. "And who might you be?"

Thomas turned and offered a nod. "Chef Thomas."

"Ah, the head chef," she purred, leaning in, obviously trying to draw attention to her chest. "How much does someone make at such a lovely restaurant?"

"Enough," Thomas replied curtly, and returned to his sizzling food.

Obviously disappointed not to be his center of attention, Heather swiveled back to Sarah and gave her a less-than-sincere smile. "So, you're doing well?"

"Yes, I'm fine." Sarah forced a steady reply. "Mom, you need to go back to the restaurant. This kitchen is just for staff."

"Ma'am, you need to leave," Juanita said, the firmness in her voice leaving no room for argument.

Heather laughed, a high, exaggerated sound that echoed off the walls. "How silly of me. I just couldn't wait to see my precious daughter. I'm going to drive around town, then visit Dot. See you tonight, sweetheart." She air-kissed Sarah's cheek before dramatically sweeping out of the kitchen, her stiletto heels echoing with each step.

Sarah's shoulders sagged, heat creeping up her neck. Why couldn't she just disappear?

Rosie moved beside her, arm draping comfortingly over Sarah's shoulders. "How your mother acts isn't your fault or your responsibility. Stand tall, Chef Livingstone. You are appreciated and loved."

The words settled around Sarah like a soft blanket, easing the sting of embarrassment. She lifted her chin and went back to her job.

Rain hammered her car's windshield as Sarah drove home. Garden Valley businesses were closed, and the streets were almost empty except for a few cars parked near the General Store.

Fearing Heather had already arrived at Dot and Ulysses' house, Sarah took deep, calming breaths to steady herself. She needed to be brave and remember that she was an adult and not responsible for her mother.

At the sight of Heather's white Lexus, a gift to her mother

by an executive she dated, parked in the driveway, Sarah groaned. She sat in her car as rain poured down her windshield like tears.

Maybe everyone would be asleep, and she could quietly make her way to her bedroom and hide from any mama drama.

Sarah dashed through the pouring rain and slipped inside the back door, shaking the water from her hair. Hearing voices, she paused in the hallway outside the family room.

"You do remember we know how to kill people," Dot's stern voice said.

"You write novels." Heather scoffed. "That's not the same."

"We know the techniques, and we practice our skills. Just ask our FBI agent."

"Sure you do. Why would *you* know anyone in the FBI?"

"Not just the FBI, we have contacts with the police, private investigators, a few people in Homeland Security, along with the CIA."

Heather's dismissive laugh made Sarah's stomach churn. "Dot, you have always been prone to exaggeration."

"Me? I write novels for a living, but you make up stories about who you are and the life you lead."

"How dare you! I can't believe you would attack me after all I've been through." Heather's shrill voice raised the hair on Sarah's arms.

"All you've been through?" Dot huffed. "The only hardship you've had in your life came from your bad choices. And what's worse, you dragged your daughter through the mud of your making."

The sharp sound of a slap echoed, followed by Heather's wail.

Sarah's breath caught in her throat, and she rushed into the room.

Dot held her hand against her already red cheek while Heather dramatically wailed as though she'd been the one struck.

Sarah's worry shifted to anger as she hurried to Dot and glared at her mother. "What did you do?"

"She insulted me!" Heather burst out in a dramatic sob. "You wouldn't believe the horrible things she said. I don't know why I even came to this house, other than to check on my baby."

Sarah squared her shoulders. "Mother, did you really come to check on me, or were you hoping I'd give you some money? That's the only reason you usually visit."

Heather rose to her full height, her dagger-like nails pointing at Sarah. "How dare you! After all I've done for you. I've taken care of you since you were born. Provided you with a home and loving care."

"You did not. You dragged me to the places where your wealthy boyfriends lived and left me to fend for myself."

Face flaming red, Heather's eyes narrowed to slits. "I cannot believe you would insult me like that. What happened to honor your mother?"

Sarah inhaled deeply, trying to quiet the scared child that trembled within her. "I am honoring my mother by telling the truth. Mom, I love you, but I'm an adult, and I am not responsible for you. You are a healthy woman who can take care of herself."

Heather fell back on the couch and clutched her chest. "I'm not a well woman. You know how I suffer with my heart problems. My doctor said so."

"Was the doctor someone you were dating or a medical professional?" Dot asked.

Heather sputtered as she rose to her feet. With a glare that could cut through steel, she approached Sarah. "I knew I should have aborted you like your other siblings. You did nothing but hinder my life. I *never* wanted you anyway." After uttering that awful statement, Heather stormed out of the room, slamming the door shut with a loud bang.

Chapter 12

Her alarm blaring, Sarah pulled the cover over her head. Last night, she'd cried until her eyes felt like sandpaper, and every ounce of water had been drained from her body.

Dot and Ulysses had surrounded her with love and comfort, even spouting Bible verses about how God had lovingly created her and had good plans for her.

If that was true, why did God put her with someone who didn't even want her?

Sarah threw back the covers and slammed her cell phone to silence the alarm app. How could she work today after what happened last night?

Still, she needed to get moving. Sarah dragged herself out of bed and into the bathroom. If only she could wash away everything that happened in her past and the terrible things her mother said.

Sarah turned on the water, let it warm up, and stepped into the shower.

She was never wanted.

With a fresh torrent of tears, she let the water wash over her. "Why, God? Why was I even born?"

I know the plans I have for you, plans to prosper you and not to harm you, plans to give you hope and a future.

The words didn't reach her ears but reverberated deep in her mind and heart.

Sarah washed and scrubbed her hair, trying to remove any insanity from her brain.

She was obviously losing her mind, or maybe it was only a replay of what Dot and Ulysses had said.

I have loved you with an unfailing love. You are mine.

The words splashed and poured into her, cocooning her heart in a deep love.

Did God really love and want her? She closed her eyes. "God, is it true? Do you love me?"

A sudden, vivid recollection overwhelmed Sarah's senses. In her mind, she was four years old again, small, trembling, and alone in a sprawling, crowded park. The memory crashed into her with such force that she doubled over, clutching her chest, as if the ache of abandonment was physical pain.

She could still taste the salt of her desperate tears, feel the panic clawing at her throat as she called for her mother over and over. Each heartbeat thundered with fear, with the crushing certainty that she was forgotten and invisible, lost in a world too big for a little girl.

Just when her hope had faded into a horrible thought that her mother had left her for good, a man had appeared. Dressed in an immaculate white shirt, his clothes glowing in the afternoon light. His eyes, the deepest blue Sarah had ever seen, met hers with such kindness that the memory still made her knees buckle. The man's smile, dazzling as the sun at midday, wrapped her in a soul-deep warmth.

Kneeling to her level, his presence was gentle and reassuring. In a voice as soft as a lullaby but resonant with strength, he promised he'd take her back to her mother.

His hand had gently gripped Sarah's as they walked side-by-side. He told her she never had to be scared or alone, because God loved her deeply and would never, ever abandon her.

He'd taken her to her mother, but when she turned to thank

him, he was gone.

Even now, years later, the memory shimmered, longing for the security she'd felt in that fleeting moment.

Tears mingled with the shower's spray as Sarah clung to the hope that, maybe, somewhere deep inside, she was still that lost little girl being found, cherished, and promised she was loved and would never be left behind.

Chapter 13

The soft whir of the office air purifiers mingled with the buzz of monitors, threatened to put Peter in a dream state.

He lifted his desk to an elevated position. He'd read that standing boosted productivity and was also much healthier than sitting, or maybe that was just what his smartwatch kept nagging him to believe.

Peter shot a sidelong glance at Quint. "I ordered flowers to be sent to Sarah today. Even selected the arrangement after trawling through countless internet lists on how to impress someone you want to get to know better. By the way, lilies are apparently neutral, but sunflowers promise that you're not a serial killer. Who knew?"

Quint's fingers drummed on his keyboard. "You're trusting the internet for romantic advice? Next, you'll be asking SAUS how to fold a fitted sheet. Not that anyone has figured out how to do that impossible task."

Peter gestured defensively at his dual monitors. "Hey, I did ask SAUS for a few ideas. I mean, if it can handle just about any question, surely it can strategize relationships, right?" He gave an upward glance. "And I've prayed. Divine wisdom always trumps algorithmic nudging."

"I wouldn't be surprised if SAUS suggested you send Sarah a bouquet of USB cables and a handwritten binary love note. Still, you're right. God knows best. Maybe He'll whisper some sense into you between code deployments."

"Well, I did what I could," Peter said. "In the card, I thanked

Sarah for the incredible food and for sharing about the restaurant. I even included my cell number."

"Good for you. And if all goes well, Sarah will call, and in a few weeks, you'll live happily ever after. But, I hate to tell you," Quint motioned with his head toward the back part of the office, "I overheard Harrison bragging he'd sent Sarah a dozen roses."

"What?" Peter rubbed his forehead. He should have thought of that sooner. Rats. He'd only sent a mixed flower arrangement. Why hadn't he sent something more extravagant?

"Stop obsessing. From Sarah's earlier reaction to Harrison, I don't think she'll be impressed by his roses. Probably will consider him a creepy stalker."

"True. She didn't seem to like his attention."

Quint gave Peter a curious look. "During your repeated visits to the restaurant, why didn't you just ask to personally thank the chef? You could have used the table-side QR code and left a five-star emoji review."

Peter internally groaned. Why hadn't he thought about that?

"You know," Quint said. "You don't have to stay out in the evenings just because Amy and I are hanging out at the house."

"Yeah, well, it's kind of awkward. Plus, when I visited the restaurant, I kept hoping Sarah would step out and I could say hello. But every time the kitchen door opened, it was a server or someone taking out a delivery."

Quint pointed to his computer screen. "Ask SAUS to communicate with Rosie's computer to put in a good word for you. AI to AI flirting."

"I'm not sure that'd be a good idea. Who knows what it would say? Something like Chef Sarah, Peter indicates he likes you. Proceed accordingly."

Quint chuckled. "AI does seem to have an interesting sense

of humor."

Peter suspiciously eyed his computer. In an office where artificial intelligence seemed to have its virtual fingerprints on everything from coffee preferences to cryptic screen messages, nothing was truly off-limits. SAUS even occasionally sent personalized reminders to drink more water or, on one memorable occasion, displayed memes featuring dancing robots whenever productivity dipped.

His monitor's camera flipped on as though SAUS were watching him. Peter taped a piece of paper over the lens to be kept safe from AI prying eyes.

A message popped up on his screen: *'Nice try, Edwards. You can never get away from my AI eye.'*

Peter squinted at his computer, then glanced over at his nemesis, Harrison, who seemed to be busy working unless he was secretly plotting against Peter with the help of his own computer assistant.

Peter typed in a coded request for SAUS to take a little harmless revenge on Harrison. SAUS, always eager to add its own quirky touch, responded immediately. Its algorithm seemed to delight in playful chaos rather than dull efficiency.

Peter wondered if SAUS would award him bonus points for creativity. Code complete and running, he picked up his coffee mug and took a casual stroll, passing the huddle room with interactive smart boards and VR setups for visual models.

Harrison narrowed his eyes as Peter approached. "Shouldn't you be working? Or are you searching for the meaning of life in your inbox again?"

Peter lifted his mug. "Just taking a coffee break."

"Sure, you're probably worried SAUS is watching you." Harrison chuckled as he leaned back in his chair.

"I knew it was you who sent that message," Peter tried to

sound serious, but it took all his strength not to crack a smile, knowing that his revenge would come soon.

"Sure you did. You're way too easy to mess with, Edwards," Harrison said. "Next time, maybe SAUS will send you a pop-up with your browser history and a romantic poem."

A shrill, high-pitched beeping erupted from Harrison's computer as a message flashed on his screen:

Warning:
Excessive Rudeness Detected.
Reboot needed for human model.
Action will be taken in five... four... three... two... one.

Harrison shoved his chair back as though SAUS might zap him.

The room broke out in laughter as Peter pumped his fist in triumph. "Got you, Miller."

Even though it had been days since what Sarah considered her God encounter, the incredible joy and hope continued. She still felt weightless, as if she were walking on air.

All around, the kitchen pulsed with energy. Chef Thomas and other kitchen staff worked on creating entrees. Servers in pressed aprons weaved between stations, their footsteps quick against the tile and their voices interwoven with friendly chatter in English and Spanish.

With the rhythmic chopping and sizzling of the restaurant kitchen in her ears, Sarah stood at the stainless steel prep surface next to Juanita as they worked on the day's dessert specials.

Sarah glanced at the table in the back where she'd placed the beautiful flowers Peter had sent. The vibrant mixed-flower bouquet bursting with color brought a smile to her face.

Juanita followed Sarah's gaze. "So, are you going to call him?"

Sarah tucked a loose strand of hair behind her ear. "Maybe."

"You're not going to call the creep who sent those, are you?" Juanita pointed to the roses that had been set aside.

"No way." Sarah wrinkled her nose. "That Harrison guy makes my skin crawl."

"If he harassed you in the restaurant, why didn't you tell one of us?"

"I didn't think it was that big of a deal." She'd been harassed before, and reporting that person hadn't gotten her anywhere.

"Maybe I'll send a text to Harrison thanking him and telling him I'm already seeing someone so he won't bother me again."

"No, don't you dare contact someone like that," Juanita warned, glancing up from her dough. "Do not call or text him. If he has your cell number, you probably wouldn't ever get rid of him."

"You need a burner phone," a waiter called as he swept past with a serving tray loaded high, the scent of carnitas trailing him out to the dining room.

Sarah turned to Juanita. "A burner phone? Like spies use?"

"Maybe your author relatives have one?"

"Good point. They might. Dot and Ulysses are always researching interesting items for their stories."

"So, back to the flowers." Juanita moved closer. "You are going to call Peter, right?"

"Yes," Sarah couldn't wait to make contact, but knowing how to respond was a different matter. "But I'm not sure what to say."

"Thank him for the flowers, and ask him to stop by this evening, and you'll give him a free dessert."

Sarah looked at her friend. "Wouldn't that be forward to offer him a bribe to come see me?"

"It's not a bribe," Juanita said with a light chuckle. "Peter sent you flowers and left you his number. He *wants* to see you."

Sarah's heart did a happy dance at that thought. But what if he was only being nice? What if he was like her last boyfriend and only wanted to use her?

She slid her tray into the oven. The hot air swirled around her, and Sarah remembered what Dot and Ulysses had shared about praise.

Sarah internally praised God that Peter had sent her flowers, and he seemed like a nice guy. She also praised God that she wasn't still in a relationship with her ex-boyfriend, and she didn't have to have anything to do with Harrison.

Tension easing from her shoulders, Sarah decided to give the roses to whoever wanted them or toss them into the trash can. And after that, she'd leave Peter a thank-you message.

Then she'd hope and pray this evening would be the start of something very sweet.

Chapter 14

After work, Peter rushed to Quint's house, took a shower so hot it nearly steamed his skin off, shaved, and made sure he looked presentable. He even dabbed on some cologne, which, he hoped, was charmingly subtle rather than overpowering.

Sarah had not only responded to his flowers, but she'd sent him a text asking if he wanted to stop in for a free dessert and a chat. He couldn't wait to get to know her better, and he was positive that any dessert she shared would rival anything he'd ever tasted.

Peter sat at the restaurant table, enjoying the tangy, slow-roasted pork and warm tortillas of his carnitas. He kept watch on the kitchen door, hoping Sarah would emerge any moment.

Since closing time was in an hour, most of the dinner clientele had already left. A couple sitting nearby and a table of teenagers didn't look like they were in a hurry. Clearly, the teenagers had discovered the secret of endless soda refills. Peter could tell the waitress, although very polite with the group, was getting antsy since she kept checking her watch every other minute.

Peter finished eating and set his plate aside. Before he came, he'd checked online, trying to figure out the proper etiquette for dating a restaurant chef. Would Sarah want to go out to eat? And exactly how could he wine-and-dine someone who worked in a kitchen making culinary masterpieces? He wasn't really into wine, and he was probably sprinting ahead by imagining she'd even be interested in him.

SAUS had suggested taking Sarah to a farmers' market, having a picnic in the park, taking a cooking class together, going to a food festival, hiking in nature, attending a symphony, and several other ideas that Peter couldn't imagine having the guts or the skill even to try. Hiking? The last time he went, he'd tripped over a tree root and invented a new move Quint had called The Flailing Flamingo.

Hopefully, if things progressed, Sarah would be honest enough to share ideas with him about how he was supposed to date a chef. Preferably, ones that did not require advanced survival or cooking skills.

His ex-girlfriend had led him around like a roped steer. Or in his case, like a man too insecure and idiotic to realize he was being used.

"Go on." Chef Thomas grinned and flicked his spatula. The hiss of the grill nearly drowned out his words.

"Are you sure?" Sarah's nerves tap-danced across her skin at the thought of meeting Peter.

"Of course." Thomas's kind gaze met hers, warm and steady. "This is probably the last order for the night."

Sarah tried to tamp down her nervousness. It wasn't like she was really going out on a date. She'd just sit and talk to Peter and see if things progressed. No pressure.

Not that she was in a hurry to get into a relationship, but it would be nice to have a male friend. That Peter was handsome and seemed kind made it even better.

Her mother said a platonic relationship with a man could never work, since going out with a man usually led to more than just talking. Sarah shuddered and mentally scrubbed the image of her mother from her brain. She didn't want to be like her mom. She wanted a sweet relationship like Dot and Ulysses, who enjoyed one another's company.

Sarah hurried to Rosie's office, where she'd stashed a pair of jeans and a cute top to wear after work. Sarah tapped on the doorframe. "Mind if I come in and get ready?"

"Not at all. I'm surprised you haven't been in sooner." Rosie grinned.

"I didn't want to leave Thomas and the others without help." Sarah's hands fidgeted with the hem of her apron.

"I'm sure they can handle things." Rosie motioned toward her private bathroom. "Feel free to take a shower if you'd like. I have shampoo, conditioner, a hair dryer, and even a fancy lotion that leaves the skin oh so soft."

Sarah thanked her, took a quick shower that felt more like a spa day crammed into five minutes, pulled her still-damp hair into a bun, changed into a different outfit, and stepped out ready to go.

Rosie grinned. "You look beautiful. Casual yet elegant. I'm sure Peter will be thrilled to see you."

"Wish me luck," Sarah said, crossing her fingers.

"Nope," Rosie shook her head, "but I will pray for you."

Sarah thanked her boss, then chose one of her favorite desserts and stepped into the dining area. Her heart thumped a rhythm only slightly faster than the restaurant's background music.

As soon as she spotted Peter, he rose to his feet, almost knocking over his water glass.

Maybe he was as nervous as she felt. Her legs a touch weak, she willed herself to walk toward him. "Hi," she said as she set the chocolate and whipped cream pastry dessert on the table.

"Hi," He greeted her with a wide smile. Peter motioned

toward the chair across the table from him, pulled it out like a gentleman, then hurried back to his place. "Thanks for agreeing to meet me."

"I appreciate the flowers and the kind note you sent," Sarah said.

"You're welcome." Peter pointed to the dessert. "And thanks for the sweet gift."

"I hope you like it."

"I'm sure I will. I enjoy everything I've had at Rosie's." Peter picked up his fork and gave it a nervous twirl, glancing her way as if asking permission to dig in. "Are you going to join me?"

"Oh, I didn't even think about that." Sarah's stomach did a nervous backflip.

"We could get another plate and fork and share."

Sarah was way too nervous to eat dessert, but Peter was still gazing at her with puppy-dog eyes, so maybe she would join him. "Okay."

Peter motioned toward his server and explained what he wanted.

Aaron, the fun-loving waiter, grinned mischievously at Sarah.

She bit back a groan. She could just imagine the good-natured banter she'd get in the morning from the staff.

Aaron delivered a plate, an extra fork, a glass of water for Sarah, and even cut the dessert in half with a flourish. "Enjoy." With a bow worthy of an Oscar, he backed away, nearly bumping into the next table.

Sarah coughed into her fist to keep from laughing out loud.

Peter chuckled as he looked toward the kitchen. "Looks like we have an audience."

When she turned around, she was mortified to find most of the kitchen staff peering through the windows.

Trying her best to ignore them, she picked up her fork and dug into the creamy, chocolaty, so-good dessert.

Peter took a bite and moaned with pleasure. "That is fantastic."

"Thank you. It's my latest creation." She resisted the urge to take a bow.

"I'm impressed. The only item I've been able to cook well is ramen. Pop it in the microwave, and presto, it's done." Peter took another bite of dessert, then wiped his mouth with a napkin. "So, tell me how you got involved in becoming a chef?"

"Long story. I had opportunities to work with cooks and chefs most of my life." At least that was one good thing her mom had given her.

"So, are you a pastry chef or a regular chef?" Peter took another bite of his dessert.

"I guess a little of both. Rosie gave me an opportunity to work in both areas. Some days I'm covered in flour. Other days, I'm surrounded by smoke from the grill."

"Carte blanche in the kitchen. You must be a master chef, then."

Sarah chuckled. "I wouldn't say that. I love working in the kitchen."

"The only kitchen work I love is eating," Peter said, patting his flat stomach.

Sarah took a bite of her food as she gathered her thoughts. "So, what exactly do you do?"

"I work with AI, aka Artificial Intelligence, training, debugging, coding, a little bit of everything. Most times, the computers are smarter than I am, but I try not to let them know."

"I can't imagine working with computers. I'm grateful for them, but clueless about how anyone can program something that makes a machine intelligent."

"I've always been interested in computers. I think it goes back to the old sci-fi TV shows with all the flashing lights. Drew me in like a bug to a bug zapper." Peter gave her an apologetic look. "Sorry, I shouldn't talk about bugs while we're eating."

"No worries." Sarah grinned." I can handle it."

Peter's smile widened further. "A woman who not only cooks, she chefs, and can handle geeky computer guys."

"Well, look who we have here." Harrison pulled out a chair next to Sarah and sat down. He leaned close to her and whispered, "When you tire of the geek, I'll take you home." His smarmy words and tone implied more than a friendly trip to drop her off at her place.

Harrison gave Peter a disgusted look. "Not sure what you're doing here, Edwards."

Peter sat straight. "I was invited, and you weren't."

Harrison glared at Peter, then flashed a smile at Sarah, the kind that made her skin crawl. He pointed at Peter. "He's not the kind of guy you should hang around. He's too bland and too geeky for someone as beautiful as you." His gaze moved from her face and rested on her chest.

Sarah's fingers tightened around her water glass, knuckles whitening as her jaw clenched. She'd been around guys like Harrison too many times and let them run all over her, but no more. "This is a private conversation. You need to leave."

When Harrison didn't budge, Sarah, with a subtle move, kind of accidentally on purpose, spilled her water on Harrison's lap.

He jolted to his feet, glaring at Peter as though it was his fault. "This isn't over, Edwards."

Grabbing a napkin, he swiped at the water stain located in a very embarrassing location. With a growl and another glare at Peter, Harrison stomped out of the restaurant.

Chapter 15

Peter tried to maintain a straight face, but the edges of his mouth kept twitching upward as he watched Harrison stalk out of the restaurant. About time someone took action against his smarmy co-worker.

While Aaron, the server, wiped the remaining water off the table, Sarah kept apologizing for what happened.

Aaron grinned. "Feel free to accidentally," he air quoted the word, "tip your water anytime you need to cool off a guy like that." He flashed another smile before disappearing into the kitchen.

The faint flush in Sarah's cheeks deepened to a rosy pink as she nervously twisted her napkin. "I probably shouldn't have done that. I'm usually a nice person."

Peter wanted to reach out to Sarah to offer comfort, but he held back since they weren't really dating. "Taking care of yourself doesn't make you a bad person. I hope my younger sisters would do the same if they were put in that kind of situation."

"You have sisters?" Sarah's gaze came up to his.

"Yep. I'm the oldest in my family, the only male with three younger sisters."

Sarah's beautiful gray eyes studied him. "You must have had an interesting childhood."

"That's an understatement. Female hormones ran rampant in our house. Probably why I was drawn to the quiet of computers. Programming a machine to do my bidding gave me power that I didn't have in a world of makeup, clothes, and dating drama."

Sarah gave him a look of amused disbelief. "Was it really that bad?"

"No. My sisters are great people. The oldest is now working in Texas, and the younger two are in college. They're great people. I'm proud of them." Peter took a last bite of his dessert, savoring the sweet flavors. "How about you? Any siblings?"

Sarah's gaze dropped to the table. "No. Just me."

Peter sensed there was more to that story and didn't want to push. He took another bite of his dessert as soft Mexican music played in the background. Waiting a few minutes, he rerouted the conversation. "So, outside of cooking, what do you enjoy doing?"

For a moment, Sarah looked confused, her brow furrowing as though she didn't know how to respond. "I enjoy reading," she finally said.

"Nice. What do you like to read?"

"My aunt and uncle are authors, Dot and Ulysses Franks, so I enjoy their stories. Their pen name is U. D. Franks. And I like romantic comedies."

Peter grinned. "I'm familiar with U. D. Franks' novels. My mom and my sisters are big fans. I've read a few myself. They're great writers."

Sarah's face lit up. "Thanks. I'll let them know you approve."

"Do your relatives live in the area?"

"Dot and Ulysses do. I'm staying with them right now."

"Good for you," Peter said." I'm staying at a buddy's house until I figure out what's next."

"Are you planning on moving?" Sarah's brow furrowed.

"No, I love my job, and Garden Valley's great. I'm just not

sure where to put down roots."

Looking deep in thought, Sarah swirled her fork on her plate. "There's a house for sale on our street, but it might be a little big for one person."

Peter gave her an appreciative nod. "I'll have to check it out. I need extra rooms for an office and guest rooms for when my family comes to visit."

"Are you close to them?"

"Yeah, I have a great family."

"Must be nice." Sarah's gaze dropped.

Warning bells went off in Peter's head. His last girlfriend had a contentious family situation, mainly because she was a spoiled brat. Sarah didn't seem that way, and her vulnerability made him want to know her more. Even so, would he want to risk moving forward?

The restaurant was now quieter. Only one other table remained, the couple laughing quietly over empty plates.

Sarah took a slow sip of water, but her faraway gaze revealed she was still lost in thought.

He'd had a great family; why couldn't he find someone with a decent past like his?

The hush of the late hour pressed in as chairs scraped softly and someone began sweeping up near the kitchen.

Peter placed his napkin on the table. "I'm sorry I kept you so long. It looks like I'd better get going so you can get home." He stood. "Thanks for meeting me. It's been great getting to know you better."

"Same here." She rose to her feet and smiled, though a shadow of worry still lingered in her eyes.

Peter gave her his best, most reassuring smile. "I hope we can get together again soon."

"I'd like that," Sarah whispered, her voice barely audible as she stared at the floor.

Peter dipped his head to get her attention and gave her another smile. "See you." He hurried out the door.

Why had he let his past girlfriend cloud the time he had with Sarah? He'd had a great time with her and then just run off.

He stopped. What an idiot. He shouldn't project how his ex-girlfriend dealt with life onto another woman.

Peter looked back at the restaurant door. He should have handled that conversation much better. Why couldn't he reprogram time and rework his responses? But in reality, no programming or coding could fix real life.

He blew out a breath, walked back to the door, jerked it open, and went back inside.

Sarah gazed at the bare plates and utensils on their table, her fingers tracing an idle pattern along the rim as she tried to hold back a flood of emotion. The conversation with Peter had been going well until they talked about family.

She drew in a shaky breath, her chest tightening. Why couldn't she move beyond her childhood? Why did those memories continue to mess with her life now? Regret and longing tangled together inside her.

"Hey," Peter walked toward her and stopped, concern etched on his face. "I'm sorry I rushed out. I've had a great night, and I really enjoyed getting to know you better. Would you be willing to consider going out with me sometime?"

Sarah smiled with relief, the tension in her shoulders loosening. "I'd like that."

"Good. I'm available whenever you have a free evening."

She tried to think of somewhere they could go on a date

that would be enjoyable yet without the pressure of too much alone time together. "The town fair is coming soon, and I'd love to go."

"Great!" Peter's smile widened. "That's a great idea. I can pick you up or meet you there."

Sarah glanced at the kitchen, where a few staff members were still looking on through the windows in the kitchen door. Being watched made her nervous, yet she tried to keep her voice steady. "Let me check the schedule, and I'll let you know."

"Thanks." Peter grinned and looked as relieved as she felt. "I look forward to it."

"Me too."

Still smiling, Peter backed away as he gave her a little wave. He bumped against a table, sending a fork clattering to the floor. He quickly picked it up, flashed a sheepish grin, and made a quick, awkward dash for the door.

Chapter 16

Needing a jolt of caffeine to shake off a lingering sense of uncertainty after his time with Sarah last night at the restaurant, Peter headed toward the break area. Family was important to him, and if Sarah had issues with hers, would that be a problem?

He inhaled the faint scent of coffee as he entered the kitchen/snack area, drawn by the promise of free snacks and the rich aroma of espresso. Working for a company on the frontlines of AI did have nice perks.

Quint, already camped at the espresso machine, glanced up as Peter entered. "How was your date with Sarah last night?"

"Good." Peter poured a cup of coffee into a double-walled paper cup. "Not sure I'd call it a date, but it went well."

Quint studied him. "You say it went fine, but I noticed a hesitation in your response."

Peter shrugged, then winced as he took a sip of his coffee, the scalding liquid burning his tongue. "Sarah's great."

"But?" Quint slid into a nearby chair.

"I don't know." Peter dropped into the seat across from him. "I don't think her childhood was as happy as mine." Donating his property and working with AI were far easier than sorting through human emotions.

Quint snorted. "Most people didn't have a family like yours. Every time you talk about them, it's all happy this and happy that. Rather disgusting, actually."

"You've never complained before."

"Of course not. Your family is amazing. That doesn't mean

everyone will be happy about that. Most people have sibling and parent drama, and many have nightmares about their childhood."

Peter met his friend's eyes, searching for truth. "You don't, do you?"

"Nah," Quint took a long sip of espresso. "It was okay. Lots I wish I could change, but I'm still standing."

Peter raised an eyebrow. "Says the man who is currently sitting."

Quint puffed out his chest with mock pride. "I'm standing on the inside." He flipped a curious gaze toward Peter. "You going to see Sarah again?"

"Yep. Next weekend we're going to the town fair."

"Great. Amy and I will be there. I plan on eating my fill of cotton candy and every fried food available."

Peter grimaced, picturing greasy fingers and sticky lips. "Hope you're planning on having antacids with you."

Quint waved off the concern. "Pffft. I have a cast-iron stomach. You should know that."

Peter chuckled, memories of Quint's notorious eating habits flickering through his mind. "I remember. You've eaten things I wouldn't squash with my shoe."

"Hey, don't insult my eating abilities. A man needs to be prepared for emergencies. And when it comes to food, I don't want to miss out or be unprepared if Earth ever reaches the zombie apocalypse stage."

"Like that's something to be worried about."

"Don't take it lightly. You never know." Quint sat back in his chair. "Word of advice. If Sarah didn't have a happy childhood, don't hold that against her."

"I wouldn't do that."

Quint leaned in, gaze steady. "Yes, you would. You've even

mentioned you didn't want to date anyone who didn't come from a nice family like yours."

Peter stiffened. "I didn't say that."

"Yes, you did."

Heat flamed up Peter's back, embarrassment prickling across his skin. He'd thought that many times, but he didn't realize he'd actually said it out loud.

Man, was he really so self-absorbed and stuck-up that he only wanted his version of a perfect woman from a perfect family? God knew he was filled with imperfections. His many failures came to mind, making him cringe.

Quint gestured with his chin toward his monitor. "Sometimes, you give SAUS more grace than you give people."

Peter winced, the sting of the words sharp as a slap. "Ouch, that hits deep."

"You talk about trusting God." Quint's expression softened. "Have you actually talked to Him about your next steps beyond where to live and work? Are you praying God directs you to the woman *He* wants you to marry? I'm not throwing stones. I need to pray more, too."

Peter blew out a shaky breath, shame tightening his chest. He appreciated his friend's honesty and directness, but the truth hurt.

He raked his hand through his hair. Man, he needed a new attitude and behavioral reprogramming. He'd been so focused on finding a woman from a good family that he hadn't prayed to become the kind of man any woman would want. He couldn't believe he'd been so shallow.

Peter stood. "Obviously, my internal source code is flawed, and I need debugging and a reboot." He pointed upward. "I'm going to sit in one of the pods and spend time with the Master Programmer."

Quint nodded. "I'll pray you get the answers you need."

"Thanks." Peter chugged his now-cold coffee and tossed the cup in the trash. Sarah had been hurt by something in her past. She needed understanding, compassion, and grace, not judgment.

Peter slipped away to have a moment of quiet with God, to beg for forgiveness for his critical attitude and for help in becoming a better man.

Tired but happy and content after another great day in the kitchen, Sarah checked her phone. Surprised that her mother had left a voicemail, Sarah hurried to her car, sat in the driver's seat, and listened to what Heather had to say.

Tears stung Sarah's eyes as Heather screamed, cursed, and insulted Sarah in every way possible, then Heather said for Sarah never to contact her again since she was a worthless, ungrateful child.

Heather's slurred speech made it clear that alcohol fueled the outburst, but still the wounds and pain from her mother's cruel words hit deep, reigniting every one of Sarah's insecurities and the heartbreak of her childhood.

Sarah pounded the steering wheel. Why didn't her mother love her? Heather preferred that Sarah call her by her first name, not "Mom" or "Mother." Probably because she didn't want to admit to any potential boyfriends that she had a daughter.

Everything Heather did was for show. She would be syrupy sweet when others were watching, but when they were alone, Heather wanted nothing to do with Sarah. She'd escape by cooking in the kitchen, watching cooking shows, or reading—

anything to stay away from Heather's volatile outbursts or cold indifference.

Movement caught Sarah's attention. Chef Thomas and Rosie exited the back door and walked to their vehicles. Sarah quickly started her car, desperate to leave before anyone caught sight of her tear-stained face.

On the drive home, the night seemed darker, her headlights dimmer as her mind ran with questions.

Why had she even been born? Why didn't Heather love her?

Sarah shot a glance upward. Where had God been all those years?

Chapter 17

Sarah swiped the tears from her swollen eyes. The torrent of cruel curses and ugly words Heather had flung at her in the voicemail still filled her mind.

Hoping no one was still awake, Sarah entered Dot and Ulysses' home and hurried down the hall.

"Is that my favorite chef?" Dot said as she walked toward Sarah.

Keeping her head down, Sarah managed a weary murmur as she hurried past Dot, desperate to escape upstairs.

"What happened?" Dot's footsteps thudded softly behind as she followed Sarah into the bedroom.

"Nothing." She threw her purse onto the bed and took a seat on the edge.

"Please tell me." Dot sat on the bed next to her.

Sarah kicked off her shoes and pushed them out of the way. "Mom called and left a message."

"I take it that wasn't a good thing."

"No." Sarah hugged her pillow to her chest. "It was awful."

"I'm so sorry." Dot gently rubbed Sarah's back. "How can I help?"

Sarah's lip trembled as she looked at her aunt. "Reverse time and let me be born to you."

Dot's eyes glistened as she wrapped her arms around Sarah and held her close. "Oh, honey, I so wish I could do that."

"Why did my mother even have me? She never wanted me." Sarah's words rasped out raw with pain.

Dot held Sarah close, then let out a shaky breath. "Your father. The man Heather was dating was already in another relationship, and I believe your mom thought if she had his baby, that he would choose her."

An icy dread ran up Sarah's spine, and she leaned away from Dot. "Was the man, my father, already married?"

Dot winced and paused for a moment. "Yes."

Wishing she could release the anger and confusion she'd carried for so long, Sarah pressed the pillow over her face and screamed.

"I'm so sorry. Your mom continues searching for love in the arms of men, but the only love that is perfect and eternal is Jesus Christ."

Sarah pulled the pillow down from her face. "Mom wants nothing to do with God or Jesus. The only time she went to church was to ditch me at Vacation Bible School in the summers for cheap childcare. God wasn't with her or with me. Heather kept moving us all over the place to be with her lovers. I've never fit in anywhere or with anyone."

Dot put an arm around Sarah's shoulder. "You don't have to fit with people. You fit perfectly with Christ."

Sarah stilled, stiffened. As much as she wanted to believe that, too many things didn't make sense. "Then where was God? Why didn't he swoop in and rescue me? I prayed so many times when I was little, begging God for help, and he didn't help me. If I wasn't at school or daycare, I was left by myself."

Dot said nothing for a long time. "I hope you don't mind me sharing an example. I've attempted your recipes, but I'm no great chef like you. But even when my cooking goes wrong, your recipe stays perfect. Even when a cake falls, the recipe is good, even if things get messy. With God, no matter how messed up a life may be, His perfect plan remains the same."

Not ready to let go of her anger, Sarah squirmed out of Dot's embrace. "A recipe is different. If God has a plan for me, I want to know what it is." Arah shot a glare at the ceiling. "And I want to know if all the pain and suffering were worth something."

"I truly believe that God never wastes our time or our pain," Dot whispered.

Sarah shoved off the bed. "Then I want God to show me.

Compassion filled Dot's eyes as she gazed up at Sarah. "Ask God. Talk to Him. Be honest with your hurt and pain. Tell Him everything you went through, everything you didn't like, and don't like. Be truthful. He already knows, but in honestly talking to God, you can let out all that has festered inside so that He can bring healing."

"Yeah, sure, that will go well. God will hate me if I tell him what I think."

"He already knows. He's a big God. He can handle it." Dot said softly, then pointed to the Bible that she'd left on Sarah's nightstand the first day she'd moved into their house. "Read the book of Psalms. If you don't know how to pray, let them be the voice for your words."

Dot gently placed her hand on the Bible. "I've done that many times when I didn't know what to say or how to pray." Her gentle and kind gaze rested on Sarah. "David wrote many of the Psalms and was very honest about the people and circumstances he didn't like. Tell God everything and then be still and listen. He wants to hear from you."

Sarah shook her head. Be honest with God? Wasn't she supposed to be cleaned up and pious, speaking in words like Thee and Thou? "You mean I can talk to God even when I'm angry and upset?"

"Even then." Dot stood and smoothed her soft hand down

Sarah's cheek. "Please don't continue to focus on the past so much that you miss the wonderful future God has planned for you. I love you. I'll be downstairs praying for you."

Waiting until Dot left. Sarah closed the door, then threw her pillow back on the bed. Fists clenched, she paced back and forth in her room. Would God hear her, and if He did, would He care?

Well, it was time to try.

She continued pacing and told God exactly what she thought. She ranted and raved, even yelling a few times, about her childhood and her mother. Surprisingly, no lightning bolt hit her, and the floor didn't open and swallow her whole.

Exhausted, Sarah crumpled onto the bed as if the mattress was the only thing keeping her from completely unraveling. For a long moment, she lay motionless, staring blankly at the ceiling, feeling raw and emptied, her breath shaky in the quiet room.

The nightstand light shone in her peripheral vision. Did Dot turn that on? Sarah rolled onto her side, the Bible bathed in a warm glow, as if beckoning to her.

Curious, she sat up and flipped through the pages until she found the book of Psalms. As she skimmed the pages, she couldn't believe how many of the chapters the author called on God to punish the wicked in some very strong language. Agreeing with the words, Sarah read a few of those out loud. Yet as she continued reading, she noticed that even when David or other writers complained, they'd still praise God.

Sarah rubbed her tired eyes. Was there something in that? Why would praising God help? That didn't make sense. Why should she praise God when He never came to her rescue?

A bookmark in the Bible caught Sarah's attention, and she flipped to the marked page in the book of 2 Chronicles, chapter twenty. Most of the chapter had been underlined.

Dot's handwritten note next to verse twenty-two said, *The power of praise!* Sarah placed the Bible on her bed, lay on her side, and settled in to read the chapter.

The verses described a giant army marching toward the nation of Judah, and the king and the people praying to God for help. The crazy thing is, the battle plan they came up with was to put the praise team out front praising God. And when they did, God defeated their enemies.

Sarah rolled onto her back and stared at the ceiling. If she stood in front of Heather and started singing praise songs, her mother would probably slap her face or have Sarah committed.

As she tried to figure out what it meant to praise God, Sarah sensed a gentle nudge, almost like a playful invitation to praise God.

But for what, exactly?

Her thoughts drifted back to the man or angel who had saved her in the park when she was four years old. Had God been there with her?

Sarah was suddenly flooded with other forgotten memories. The daycare worker, who had brushed Sarah's hair and given her extra hugs. The Vacation Bible School workers who made her feel special. The teacher who helped Sarah with algebra. The nice girl in her high school who made Sarah feel welcome at a new school, and the friendly neighbors at the various places she'd lived.

Sarah closed her eyes as more and more memories came. The love Dot and Ulysses had given Sarah throughout her life, and the way they opened their home and made her feel welcomed and loved. The reality of reaching her goal as a chef at a great restaurant. Even Peter's face came to mind.

Then she remembered the time in the shower, when she'd sensed God sharing His love. Sarah groaned. Why had she so quickly forgotten that? Why did she allow what Heather said and did to affect her so easily?

Sarah stilled as another thought came. If Heather hadn't moved them around to so many places, Sarah would never have met the people she did and worked with all those amazing restaurant chefs. Perhaps God hadn't forgotten her, and she had reasons to praise Him after all.

Gazing up at the ceiling, Sarah's mind transformed it into an endless expanse of midnight sky, dazzling with countless stars twinkling above her. A soothing tranquility wrapped her in a gentle, comforting embrace, quieting her racing heart and filling her with a deep sense of peace.

She offered a prayer of thanks to God for helping her through tough times, including those involving her mother, and prayed that God would help and guide her through whatever came next.

Chapter 18

The morning light poured into her bedroom window, and Sarah, still half-asleep, stretched and wrapped her robe around her. Today was a new day with new possibilities. She whispered a prayer of thanks as she walked down the stairs.

The enticing aroma of cinnamon and coffee made her stomach rumble in anticipation. Entering the kitchen, Sarah smiled at her uncle sitting at the table. "Morning."

"Good morning," Ulysses raised his coffee cup in greeting. "I hope you slept well last night."

"I did." Sarah poured coffee into her favorite mug with a charming cartoon chef with a rolling pin in his chubby hands.

"Dot told me about what happened. I'm sorry."

"Yeah, that wasn't very pleasant." Sarah sat across from him at the kitchen table. "I hate how Heather acts, but I spent time with God last night and feel better."

"Good for you. That's the best time any of us can spend." Ulysses laid his hand on hers. "We're grateful you're here with us. And we aren't kidding when we say we want to adopt you."

Sarah puffed out a laugh. "Don't you think I'm a little old for that?"

He softly squeezed her hand before letting go. "You're never too old to be a part of our family."

Her heart squeezed. If only that were reality, and she was really their child. "I wish that were true."

Ulysses, smiling, stared at her for a moment. "Well, anyway. I hope you don't mind, but after Dot mentioned Heather's message, I did some online investigating. I suspect her reason for contacting you is that she's dating someone again. Her social media feed is overflowing with romantic pictures of them on some Caribbean island getaway. I believe she's trying to keep her grown daughter a secret from her latest boyfriend."

Sarah sighed. "Unfortunately, that makes sense. That's why she shipped me to your house for weeks at a time."

"We were always glad to have you here."

"Ulysses, have you seen my red pen?" Dot entered the kitchen, the object sticking up behind her ear.

He grinned and pointed. "Check your right side."

Dot patted her head and took the pen in her hand. "Ah, there you are, my little red beauty." She turned her gaze to Sarah. "How are you feeling this morning?"

"I'm good. Thanks for last night's advice. I spent time talking, or should I say ranting, at God. He didn't zap me with a lightning bolt, so I read the account you had bookmarked about the praise team going before the army and God destroying their enemies. Which I still think is incredibly odd. But after that, I started praising God, and I slept better than I have in a long time."

"When I felt my lowest," Dot said as she sat at the table, "all I could do was thank God for the sunshine. It sounded silly, but it helped me break through the darkness I was feeling inside."

"Praise is a powerful weapon against the devil and our own thoughts," Ulysses said. "By praising God, we turn our attention away from our difficulties and toward our all-powerful God."

Sarah sat back in her chair. "Maybe I need to try that." She took a drink of her coffee, amazed that she was actually comfortable having a discussion like this without getting upset. A new understanding of God brought her a sense of inner peace, more profound than she'd ever known.

"I've got a wonderful breakfast ready." Dot removed a tray from the oven and held it toward them.

Sarah laughed. "You bought my Sopapilla cinnamon churro bites."

Dot gave a cheesy grin. "I told you it would be wonderful."

After breakfast and a sweet time with her relatives, Sarah prepared for work, then checked her phone.

Peter had sent three messages. She laughed out loud at the cute messages he'd sent. Sarah took a few minutes to decide on a reply she hoped would be funny, then typed her response.

Only a moment later, Peter's text beeped on her phone. She chuckled at his fun response and sent him another text thanking him, but she needed to get to work. His quick reply was a funny emoji.

Two hours later, Sarah was still smiling after last night's marathon praise session, the sweet morning with Dot and Ulysses, and Peter's adorable texts.

She stood next to Thomas at the grill. The smoky air danced around them, carrying the rich smell of meat, peppers, and onions.

One of the waitresses skidded to a stop next to Sarah. "There's a cute guy out there who wants to thank the female chef for the wonderful meal."

Sarah gave Thomas a hopeful glance. "Permission to leave for a few minutes?"

Thomas, brandishing a spatula like a scepter, grinned. "Go, Chef. I've got you covered."

She stripped off her apron, checked her reflection in the kitchen's steel fridge, and dashed into the employee bathroom for a quick lipstick rescue.

Sarah practically floated through the swinging doors, only

to come to a screeching halt.

Harrison, looking like he'd just stepped out of a tech-bro catalog, stood and flashed what he probably thought was a dazzling smile. "Chef Sarah, I'd like to personally thank you for the wonderful meal." He moved in closer. "Emphasis on personally."

From his skin-crawling smile, she understood completely what he meant. Noticing the curious eyes of the lunch crowd pretending not to eavesdrop, she plastered on her politest restaurant smile. "I'm glad you enjoyed the food. I'll pass your compliments to the team."

Sarah turned to head back to the safety of the kitchen.

Harrison grabbed her arm. "Wait." He leaned in close enough that she could smell the salsa on his breath. "If you decide not to allow me to," his gaze swept down to her chest and back to her face, "personally thank you, I can make life very uncomfortable for Peter."

Heat flaming up her back, Sarah forced herself to be brave and brushed his fingers off her arm. "Are you threatening Peter and trying to blackmail me?"

Harrison shrugged as though it shouldn't matter. He'd obviously gotten away with that kind of behavior before. "With a few extra lines of code, I could ruin Peter's reputation in an instant." He snapped his fingers, his lips curling in a way that sent shivers down her spine. "Unless you choose wisely and go out with me later this evening." He didn't even keep his voice quiet, as though it didn't matter if anyone heard.

Sarah fisted her hands, trying to calm herself and slow her rapid breathing. Her mother controlled her life with a constant stream of intimidation and manipulation. But no more. Not from Heather or anyone else. She refused to tolerate threats from Harrison.

This restaurant and Dot and Ulysses' home were her safe places. God had helped her through her childhood, and He would help her now. Praise God that she was an adult and didn't have to put up with intimidation from anyone.

Sarah stood as tall as she could. "I *will* report your threats to management."

Harrison, still smiling, shrugged like it wouldn't do any good.

She turned and, on slightly trembling legs, walked back into the kitchen and straight to the employee bathroom. Shutting the door behind her, Sarah steadied herself against the sink and sent up a silent torrent of praise to God, hoping He would act against the enemy coming against her and Peter.

Taking steadying breaths, Sarah went to Rosie's office to report Harrison's threats to ensure the safety of herself and any of the other employees.

"Sarah, you did exactly the right thing coming to me," Rosie said, her tone both gentle and fierce. "No one should have to put up with that kind of behavior, especially not from someone who thinks he can intimidate you or anyone else."

Sarah nodded, relief mingling with lingering anxiety. "Thank you, Rosie. He threatened Peter, too."

Rosie's eyes flashed with anger. "Let him know what Harrison said. I will not allow you or anyone else to be threatened in this restaurant. I'll talk to the staff. If Harrison comes back, he will be escorted out of the building and permanently banned from the premises. And if you ever feel unsafe again, you come find me, no questions asked."

Sarah managed a grateful smile. "Thanks, I appreciate that."

Rosie gave her a reassuring squeeze on the shoulder. "You're part of my team, and that means you don't have to face this alone. And, Sarah, I'll ask around and find out if our staff or any of the customers heard what happened."

Sarah thanked her, then rushed to her phone and sent a warning text to Peter to let him know Harrison would be on the warpath.

Peter's jaw clenched as his fingers gripped his phone. He slid it across the table to Quint. Without a word, he jabbed at the message from Sarah, forcing himself to hold back a surge of words as his friend leaned in to read.

"I can't believe Harrison threatened Sarah and you," Quint growled. "No, wait, I can."

"At least Sarah reported what happened to her boss. Harrison's now banned from the restaurant." Peter was proud of Sarah's bravery in reporting the incident, but furious that she'd been harassed. If only he could write a programming code that would keep her safe. She didn't seem to realize how beautiful and amazing she was.

"I think more action needs to be taken," Quint said as he typed on his keyboard. "It's time we let SAUS know the kind of tech guy Harrison is."

Peter put his phone back in his back pocket. "As though SAUS would care. AI has its own agenda. Learn, grow, and take over the world."

"Probably." Quint pointed toward the server room. "But for now, SAUS needs us and needs to know who to trust."

Peter squinted at the computer screen. "What would you tell AI about this?"

Quint held up his hand. "Leave it to me. SAS and I have an understanding. We will handle the situation."

Chapter 19

"I don't know about this." Peter gazed around the office before moving his chair closer to Quint. "Harrison drives me crazy and harasses most of the women he comes into contact with, but make sure you don't have SAUS do anything unethical or immoral."

Quint gave him a look, a mixture of bewilderment and amusement. "I wouldn't allow that. However, SAUS has come up with several interesting ideas, such as banishing Harrison to a submarine or a remote monastery, or sending him to work in the office of an all-male prison. SAUS even suggested a monastic region in Greece that has banned women, including female animals, for over 1,000 years."

Peter didn't know whether to laugh or cringe. The AI's plans seemed ridiculous, and he felt uncomfortable considering letting a machine determine someone's punishment, no matter what they did. "Those sound pretty extreme."

"I agree," Quint said. "So another option is to send Harrison's resume to another job opportunity in a remote northern location far away from you and Sarah. Imagine Harrison in a place where he can't bother anyone. Still, I get what you're saying. We need to be careful. Power like this shouldn't be abused."

Quint's fingers hovered above the keyboard, his brow furrowed. "Sometimes, I wish we could just call him out face-to-face. But you know how slippery he is. AI might be our only shot at making sure people like him don't keep getting away with their behavior."

"I don't know." Peter was torn between wanting justice for Sarah and fearing that intervening with AI could cross ethical lines. "Wait, just how northern is this job?"

"Close to the North Pole for AI research on climate modeling, autonomous drones for ice exploration, data analysis, even penguin tracking." Quint grinned. "What's not to love?"

"Why would Harrison take a job like that?" Peter whispered. He wanted justice, not exile.

Quint leaned back, shrugging with a half-smile. "If Harrison thinks this job will get him ahead, he'll jump at it, even if it means freezing his tail off." Quint's lips twisted in a wry grin. "Let's hope he likes penguins."

Peter tapped his pen against his desk. "If Sarah worked here, she could go straight to human resources. But how do we report something Harrison did outside the company? All I have is Sarah's text saying what happened."

"Harrison not only harassed Sarah, but he also threatened you by saying that with a few extra lines of code, he could ruin your reputation. Threats like that aren't to be taken lightly. Those could affect you both and the company. It's just a shame there isn't more proof."

"What's an even bigger shame is that he's getting away with that kind of behavior. Wait. What if Rosie's has cameras in the restaurant? Wouldn't that show what Harrison did?"

"Maybe. But it wouldn't pick up the conversation."

"True." Peter slumped in his chair. From the start of the AI model's development, He'd worked on reinforcement learning to make sure the AI model accessed current, relevant, and reliable information before answering questions. He'd even carefully formulated biblical principles to guide SAUS in making the right choices and recommendations for humans.

However, technology could never replace the moral courage needed to address injustice head-on. Peter got his game face on and stood. "I'm going to let our team leader and Human Resources know what Harrison said."

Quint regarded him with a look of respect. "Good for you. You need to protect Sarah, yourself, and the company."

Peter looked over to where Harrison sat at his workplace. "After that, I'm going to let him know that I reported him."

Quint's eyebrows shot up. "You sure you want to do that? He is bigger than you are."

Peter straightened his glasses and his resolve. "Doesn't matter. I will not ignore the issue. But while I'm gone," he kept his voice low. "I wouldn't mind if SAUS sent that job offer to Harrison."

"On it," Quint said as his fingers flew across the keyboard.

Peter's phone vibrated in his back pocket. He took it out and stared at a message from Sarah that included a video recording. He couldn't believe it. He let out a relieved laugh. "Looks like we might have gotten a big break."

Peter showed Quint the video message. "A customer sitting close by witnessed the scene, recorded Harrison's threats to Sarah, and then sent the video to the restaurant owner, who then sent it to Sarah."

Quint smiled. "The audio isn't great, but you can still hear Harrison's threats. Looks like he's finally been caught."

"And it's time to make sure that trap is shut tight." Peter straightened his back and walked to Human Resources.

Thirty minutes later, he hurried to Quint's desk and sat near his friend, keeping his voice low. "Evidently, our co-worker was already on a final warning for earlier harassment charges."

"I'm not surprised. Good thing you had the video and reported what happened," Quint said. "Sounds like the company will be looking for a replacement soon. I did have SAUS send the northern job offer to Harrison's inbox. I believe there is a 99.98% probability he will jump at the offer in the frozen north."

"I hope so. I want him gone from the company and the area. Wish me luck. I'm going to let Harrison know that his actions have been reported." Peter squared his shoulders, feeling both adrenaline and dread churn in his gut, he walked to where his co-worker was staring at his computer monitor.

Harrison shot him a disgusted look, his lip curling with contempt. "What do you want, Edwards?"

Peter's heart pounded against his ribcage, but he kept his voice steady. "What you said to Sarah is despicable, making threats against her and me if she didn't go out with you."

"Why would I say something like that?" Harrison's reply slithered out, reminding Peter of a snake poised to strike. "I'm sure she must be mistaken."

Peter really wanted to hit the man, but he forced his fists to unclench. The fluorescent lights seemed to buzz louder in his ears as he brought his phone out of his back pocket.

He navigated to the video and set it on the desk in front of Harrison. "There's no mistake. I've reported your actions to our team leader and Human Resources."

Harrison's face turned ashen, all the bravado draining away as he watched the footage.

"HR is on the way to escort you to their office and then out of the company."

"They wouldn't do that." Harrison glared at him.

Peter pointed to the doorway.

Harrison's gaze shot to the HR manager and team leader walking toward them. His eyes widened, and a tremor of disbelief flickered across his expression.

Peter's earlier adrenaline drained away as he watched

Harrison escorted out of the office. Peter's legs feeling somewhat rubbery, he stumbled to where Quint waited and collapsed next to his friend.

"Looks like the problem has been appropriately handled," Quint said with a satisfied smile.

"Yes, it does." Peter took out his phone and texted Sarah, letting her know that Harrison had been fired.

Sarah's reply lit up his cellphone screen with her grateful comments, a smiley face emoji, and a promise that she looked forward to going with him to the town fair.

He sighed with relief. A few days from now, he'd be enjoying his evening with a beautiful woman far from AI and co-worker troubles.

Chapter 20

The scent of sweet kettle corn and cotton candy in the air, Sarah breathed deep. Walking alongside Peter, their hands would occasionally touch as they strolled through the bustling Garden Valley town fair.

The blocked downtown streets buzzed with activity. Stalls from local businesses and crafters offered food, flowers and potted plants, stained-glass creations, handmade quilts, ceramics, folk art, and local produce. Lively music came from the gazebo area.

"Thank you again for helping with the Harrison... issue," Sarah said.

"You're more than welcome. I'm sorry you were subjected to his harassment." The tenderness in Peter's voice pressed deep into her heart. "You don't have to worry about Harrison anymore. He was spotted yesterday buying a parka from Shaffer's Outfitters."

Confused, Sarah stared at Peter. "A parka?"

"I believe Harrison will be miles away from here. So unless you decide to live in the Arctic, you'll be safe."

"I'm more than happy to stay here."

"Good." Peter's sweet smile warmed her cheeks and her heart.

Sarah stopped to watch a street artist paint a portrait of a young girl. The man's talent was simply astonishing.

Peter stood beside her. "He's really gifted. I wonder if he's the one putting in the art gallery?" He motioned toward one of the older downtown buildings being refurbished.

"That would make sense. I've never seen someone work that fast and yet create such an incredible, lifelike portrait."

"Maybe he's in disguise and is actually the famous painter that's on TV," Peter whispered.

Sarah grinned. "I doubt he would come here. Plus, the man you're talking about has passed away."

Peter clutched his chest. "No. Say it isn't so."

By the sparkle in his brown eyes, she knew he was teasing.

Peter scanned the area. "Looks like most of the town turned out. Reminds me of when my dad used to take us to the county fair."

"This is my first one." Sarah hoped her voice didn't sound too wistful. She'd always wanted to go to one, but Heather never had an interest in anything that didn't put her in contact with wealthy men.

"Really? You never got to go to one?" A shadow of concern crossed Peter's face before his smile returned. " I'm honored to be your escort." He crooked his elbow in front of her like a gentleman in a historical novel.

She placed her hand on his arm. "Thank you, kind sir. Lead on."

He gestured toward a nearby stand where bright yellow jars caught the fading sunlight. "Might I tempt you to sample a honey stick, milady?"

It took Sarah a moment to figure out how to reply in a way that stayed in character. "It would please me greatly."

Peter stopped and courteously bowed. "Pray pardon me, my lady. Would you care for a heartier meal before indulging in such sweetness?"

"I do believe a touch of honey before we dine would be most agreeable."

Peter led her to the honey booth, hesitated briefly with a puzzled expression, then leaned toward her. "I'm not sure I can keep this kind of dialogue up for much longer."

Sarah chuckled. "I'm with you. It's difficult enough to form regular sentences, let alone speak like they did in earlier times."

A few minutes later, their sweet treats in hand, they walked again along the street. The warmth of the summer evening mingled with a gentle breeze.

"Peter!" A silver-haired gentleman in a veteran's baseball cap hurried toward him. "I can't thank you enough for what you've done for our vets."

"You're more than welcome." He shook the man's outstretched hand. "I hope it's going well."

"It's been a blessing. We are very grateful for what you did."

"God gets all the credit."

The man clapped him on the back. "You're so right. Stop over and see us sometime."

"Yes, sir. I'll do that."

"Well, thanks again." The man's gaze passed from Sarah back to Peter. "Enjoy your evening."

Sarah watched with curiosity. Had Peter donated money to the group? She touched his arm to get his attention. "What was that about?"

Peter shrugged a shoulder. "Nothing much." His smile returned as he turned toward her. "Why don't we keep exploring?"

As they continued their stroll, Sarah spotted a booth where Dot and Ulysses had a table to sell their novels. She dearly loved her relatives but wasn't sure she wanted Peter to be subjected to their quirky humor.

Thankfully, Peter pointed in another direction. "I'm not sure whether to call that a ride, an attraction, or what it is."

Sarah fought back a chuckle at the sight of the golf cart pulling what appeared to be a train of brightly colored plastic oil drums. The sounds of squeals and laughter came from the children riding the supposed train.

"Unless you want to ride," Peter said with a cute grin. "I suggest heading this way." He motioned toward the gazebo.

Strings of glowing lights crisscrossed above the area where a band played music ranging from slow to fast-paced.

Sarah stood next to Peter, watching young children and older adults twirling and dancing to the music, with the occasional toddler spinning out of control and nearly colliding with a startled teenager.

"Care to dance?" Peter asked.

Sarah shook her head. "I'm not that good."

"I didn't ask you if you danced well. I want to know if you would join me since I have two left feet."

She grinned. "Then you're my kind of dance partner."

He led her onto the designated area, and their attempt at a waltz quickly turned into what could be described as creative freestyle.

They narrowly dodged two teenagers engaged in what looked like a playful form of slam dancing. At one point, Peter spun Sarah straight into a giggling group of kids, who cheered as if it were all part of the show.

Slightly dizzy from the spin, Sarah giggled. "At this rate, we'll be banned from all small-town dances."

"Don't worry," Peter grinned. "I've been banned before. It's tradition."

In the middle of the dance, they collided with another pair, and Peter, without missing a beat, introduced Sarah to Quint, his friend, and to Amy, Quint's girlfriend.

Smiles and laughter were exchanged as everyone kept

dancing, careful to keep their toes and dignity mostly intact.

Sarah's cheeks hurt from smiling so much. She hadn't had this much fun since dancing with Dot and Ulysses.

A slow song started, and Peter gave her a puppy-eyed, hopeful look. "Would you mind?"

She matched his smile. "A slow song would be nice."

Peter took her in his arms, his heartbeat a steady rhythm as she lay her head on his shoulder. Beneath the gentle glow of the lights, she felt like Cinderella in the arms of her prince.

The song was over much too soon, leaving Sarah wishing she could bottle the feeling of being close to Peter. She reluctantly took a step back, but the warmth of his arms lingered like a soft blanket.

He took her hand in his. "Mind if I buy you some food?"

"Thank you. I'd like that."

Peter led her off the dance floor, dodging a sticky spilled soda. He stopped at the stall offering corn dogs, its neon sign blinking. "I can take you to a nice restaurant for dinner, or we can eat something more adventurous." His grin reminded her of a mischievous kid begging for candy.

"I'll give it a try." She'd eaten a few corn dogs in school lunchrooms. They weren't her favorite food, but maybe what they had here would be more appetizing.

"Great! I haven't had one of these since the last time I went to a county fair. Want French fries too?"

"Sure. Might as well go straight for the cholesterol juggler." Sarah imagined her arteries whimpering and raising little white flags.

Peter hesitated as he looked at the food booth and then back at her. "I'm sorry. This might not be the best food to eat after dancing."

Sarah chuckled. "I don't think it will be a problem." Her

stomach grumbled in agreement.

Peter shoved a hand through his hair, making it stick up at odd angles. "I should take you somewhere nice. White tablecloths, steaks, the works. You deserve the best."

"I don't think I deserve anything. Corn dogs and fries will only make me stronger." Sarah flexed her arm.

"I'm glad you didn't say it would put hair on your chest. Not that I was thinking about your chest—I mean, oh, man." His face flamed beet red, and he cringed as if wishing the concrete would open up and swallow him whole. He groaned and cleared his throat. "Sorry about that. I'm saying and doing all the wrong things. Computers are easier than people."

"Cooking is easier for me."

"Tell you what. You cook, I'll code, and we'll take our chances at fried food. However, I would love to take you somewhere nice for dinner sometime."

Sarah smiled. "I'd love that too."

"Good. It's a date. Or at least, we'll set a date and time for later." He shook his head as though to clear his thoughts. "I'll place our order." He pointed to an empty table speckled with ketchup and mustard packets. "Want to wait for me?"

"Of course I'll wait." Happier than she'd been in a long time, Sarah sat at the table, her senses alive with the sights, sounds, and savory scents of the town fair.

Sarah recognized a customer from the restaurant walking with his family. Melba, who worked at the soda counter in the grocery store, waved as she hurried past. At a nearby booth, Sarah spotted a farmer who provided produce for Rosie's restaurant.

She sighed a happy sigh. Garden Valley was definitely a good place to be.

Sarah turned back to watch Peter standing in line. An

attractive blonde-haired woman came up behind Peter and tapped him on the shoulder. "Don't you work at SAU Tech?"

Peter turned toward her and smiled. "Yeah. I've seen you before. You work in marketing, right?"

"That's right. We'll have to get together sometime." Her flirty smile made her intentions obvious.

Peter's gaze darted toward Sarah and then back to his co-worker. "I'm sure we'll see each other at work." He turned back to the counter and placed their order.

The woman stared at his back for a moment, then straightened her shoulders and walked away.

Sarah stared at a dark spot on the table. No telling how many pretty women worked at his office. Why did she ever think she would have a chance with someone as sweet and handsome as Peter? And why couldn't she shake off her insecurities?

Chapter 21

Peter placed the paper food trays with corn dogs and salty fries on the table.

Without looking up, Sarah murmured her thanks.

He sat across from her and couldn't help but notice that something seemed to be bothering her.

Was she upset over his awkward joke about corn dogs putting hair on her chest? He hadn't meant anything by his ill-timed statement, but he shouldn't have said something like that to Sarah. He'd been raised to treat women with respect. His mom would clean his mouth with soap.

Or was Sarah upset about the cheap food? Or maybe because of the flirty encounter he'd had with his coworker a few minutes ago?

Peter inwardly groaned because he didn't have any idea what Sarah was upset about. People were far harder to read than computer code. According to his previous girlfriend, he was clueless. She would ignore him for weeks if she disapproved of his actions.

He purged those unpleasant thoughts from his mind. He needed to focus on Sarah and figure out what was troubling her. He touched her arm. "Are you okay?"

Sarah looked up, her gray eyes clouded with something he couldn't quite place. "Oh, yeah. Sure." She gave a small smile and plucked a fry from the tray.

Peter leaned forward, voice lowered. "I'm not great at picking up on feelings or what people are thinking. I'm sorry if

I said or did something wrong."

Her shoulders sagged as she shook her head. "No, it's not you," she whispered.

If it wasn't something he did, what was he supposed to do or say? "If you were hoping for Fred Astaire on the dance floor, I'm sorry that you got a computer geek with two left feet and questionable food choices." He pointed to the corn dogs.

Sarah's lips twitched, but she didn't quite smile. "No, your dancing was wonderful, the food's fine, and you..." She hesitated, glancing up at him. "You're wonderful. Sometimes I just get insecure." Her voice was small, vulnerable in a way that made Peter's heart ache.

He reached for her hand. "Sarah, you're beautiful, fun, talented, and the most amazing woman I know."

She blinked, tears pooling. "Me?" Her voice squeaked.

"Yes, you." He gently squeezed her fingers. "Sarah Livingstone, you're incredible."

Her wary gaze searched his as though she didn't believe what he'd said. "Thank you."

Peter couldn't believe Sarah didn't realize her beauty. He'd noticed other men's eyes following her as they walked by. He sensed something more in Sarah Livingstone's insecure gaze that he couldn't quite understand.

While they ate, Peter racked his brain for a way to show her beauty. An idea popped into his head. "After we finish eating, I want to show you something."

Her questioning gaze flicked to his for a moment. "Okay."

Once they finished, Peter led Sarah to a booth where the local artist sat with his pad, capturing the likeness of an older woman in bold, sure strokes.

Peter leaned in to the artist and quietly explained Sarah's insecurities, asking the man to show her how beautiful she really was.

The man gazed at Sarah for a moment, smiled, then nodded at Peter.

A few minutes later, Sarah sat stiffly on the stool as the artist worked, her eyes darting nervously between Peter and the crowds moving around them.

Finally, the artist finished and motioned for Peter. "What do you think?"

Peter's breath caught at the drawing of Sarah as a regal, radiant princess, her long brown hair framing her face, and her gray eyes filled with a warm light.

Delighted with the finished product, Peter slipped the artist extra money.

The man stood and handed the portrait to Sarah.

She gasped, tears shimmering in her eyes. "This is me?"

Both Peter and the artist nodded.

Wide-eyed, Sarah stared at the portrait. As she studied the picture, Peter noticed a slight lifting of Sarah's shoulders, as though finally seeing herself through someone else's loving eyes.

With the portrait nestled securely in a canvas bag, Sarah walked close to Peter. The artist's depiction of her as a princess seemed surreal. The soft paper covering the portrait was probably the nearest she'd ever come to becoming royalty, but for now, she clung to the feeling it gave her.

From the gazebo, a guitarist's melody drifted on the evening air. The notes strummed with aching sweetness, mingled with laughter and the hum of conversation. A crowd of people, some standing, others sitting in lawn chairs, tapped their feet to the song, while still others danced.

The music wrapped around Sarah, warm and inviting as Peter guided Sarah to an open bench.

She sat, feeling the gentle brush of Peter's shoulder against her. As the musician's voice soared, singing stories of heartbreak and hope, Sarah let herself sink into the moment.

Peter's eyes were closed as though he was letting the music fill his soul. He was such a nice guy, but she'd trusted another man before, and that didn't turn out well. Could she trust Peter?

He turned, his gaze meeting hers. "So, what do you think of your first town fair?"

"It's been wonderful," she replied, meaning every word.

"This is my favorite fair." Peter nudged her with his shoulder. "All because of you." His gaze dropped to her lips and then back to her eyes as though wondering if she would mind.

Sarah's stomach fluttered at the thought. She wouldn't mind a kiss from him, not at all.

"Sarah!" Dot's voice called as she bustled toward them with Ulysses trailing behind. Her mischievous grin bounced to Peter before settling on Sarah. "Who's your friend?"

He stood, his easy smile returning. "Peter Edwards."

Ulysses shook his outstretched hand. "Ulysses Franks, and this is my wife, Dot."

"U. D. Franks," Peter said with a touch of awe. "It's an honor to meet you both."

"You're familiar with our books?" Dot practically swooned at the mention of their novels.

Sarah bit back a smile at Dot's theatrical delight. Her relatives always managed to bring laughter, even at awkward moments.

"Yes, ma'am," Peter replied. "My sisters are big fans, and I've also enjoyed your stories."

"Ah, you are a man of great taste." Dot's smiling gaze swept back to Sarah.

Sarah kept herself from rolling her eyes at their untimely appearance and fun comments.

Dot nudged her husband. "We'd better get going and let them enjoy their evening."

"Right. Yes," Ulysses stammered. "Okay, good to meet you, Peter. Take good care of our girl."

"Yes, sir. I will." Peter chuckled as he sat down next to Sarah again. "It was nice to meet your relatives."

"They are entertaining," Sarah puffed out a laugh at the wild stories and eccentricities of her author relatives.

"I can't imagine living with authors. Do they role-play their stories, discuss their plots, and do their characters live in their heads?"

Sarah shook her head, grinning. "You have no idea how crazy it is with those two. But they're so sweet to me."

Peter's gaze searched hers. "I'm glad to know you're being well taken care of."

"Yes, they spoil me. I just wish they'd been my parents." Sarah cringed. She didn't mean to say that out loud.

Peter's warm fingers curled around hers. "I don't know all you've been through, but if you ever want to talk, I'm here."

The gentleness in his words and touch sent a rush of emotion through Sarah. "Thank you," she whispered, meaning it with all her heart.

"I hope Garden Valley is a good place, somewhere you'll want to stay." Peter leaned in, and his lips brushed hers with a soft kiss.

Sarah kissed him back, her body melting into the warmth and security of his embrace. A sense of belonging rose within her. Maybe, just maybe, she'd found a place to call home.

Cook, Code, and a Leap of Faith

Chapter 22

With the evening crowd winding down at the restaurant, Sarah hurried to finish the last orders.

She and Peter had been officially dating for four months. Between their work schedules, they'd spent practically every moment together.

The argument with Peter last night replayed in her mind. Her words had tumbled out faster than she meant, accusing him of being too perfect for someone as imperfect as her. He'd laughed at first, then winced, and quickly apologized. He didn't think she'd been serious.

Peter had taken her into his arms and assured her he was a man of many failures, even admitting to some of his cringeworthy moments. He was human after all.

She'd never known anyone like Peter. He'd even developed an app for her phone to use for her recipes, proving her point that he was an exceptional man.

Every moment they spent together, she loved him more. Not that she'd said the words out loud to him. Oh, she'd wanted to many times, and he'd told her he loved her, but for some reason she kept holding back.

Was she afraid she'd jinx their relationship since the last guy she told she loved had sabotaged her heart and her job?

She needed to remember Peter was different. He was loved by Dot, Ulysses, the restaurant staff, and just about everyone they knew. Sarah glanced at the clock. Peter was coming this evening to join her for a late dinner.

"Go," Thomas grinned as he waved his spatula. "Your man is waiting."

Her man. Sarah smiled at the thought. Why couldn't she admit she loved Peter?

After a quick freshening up, she brought out the dinner they were going to share along with her latest salsa concoction.

She set the mason jar in front of him. "It will make hair grow on your chest."

Peter chuckled. "You're never going to let me forget that comment, are you?"

She sat next to him. "Nope." She picked up her salsa creation and sighed. "I could drink it in one swig."

"No, you wouldn't, would you?"

She stuck a chip in the salsa and brought it up with a massive amount of the spicy condiment. "The more, the better."

"I'm impressed." Peter took a bite of his meal and moaned in pleasure. "I love that I'm dating a chef."

Sarah pretended to be hurt. "You only love me for my cooking?"

Peter shook his head. "No, I love you because you are you."

Her heart hammered in her chest as she stared into Peter's eyes. She wanted to say the words, tell him she loved him, but with the restaurant customers around them, it didn't feel quite right. Not here. Not now.

Peter stabbed his food with his fork. "Next evening when you're off, I vote we do something other than play games."

Sarah smiled at the memories of the fun game nights with her relatives. "You're just mad that you lost at Charades."

"Playing with the famous duo of U.D. Franks is not fair. I think they know every subject and charade move under the sun." Peter grumbled.

"Now you know how I feel when we play video games at

Quint's house. I couldn't even drive a car in a kid's game."

"You're adorable when you play and when you pout." Peter's smile softened as his fingers brushed Sarah's hand, shooting a thrill through her.

"I'm not pouting."

"Says the woman whose lower lip is pushed out a touch." Peter's eyes glimmered as he leaned closer. "Which I don't mind at all since that makes you even more kissable."

He made a kissy sound, causing Sarah's cheeks to flush with embarrassment. "Please, not here."

"You didn't seem to mind the other evening." Peter grinned.

"We were in a private place," Sarah whispered.

"True. Other than Quint and Amy were in the family room while we hid in the kitchen pantry."

Heat running up her back at the pleasant memory, Sarah grinned. "Good thing he has a big pantry."

"Finding time alone with you is getting more and more difficult, but it does keep us out of trouble." A touch of Peter's hand on her arm sent happy goosebumps rippling across her skin.

Her mind went blank for a few minutes before she could form any words. "Thank you for not taking things too far."

Peter let out a long sigh. "You are extremely kissable and incredibly sexy. However, my parents raised me to be a gentleman, but that doesn't mean it's easy."

Sarah fanned her face. "No, it's not."

"You find me irresistible?" Peter's grin bordered on cheesy and saucy.

"Yes, because I love you."

Peter rocketed out of his chair. "She loves me!"

Applause broke out around them. Embarrassment heat igniting her body, Sarah considered diving under the table and hiding. Why did she tell him now?

She loved him! Peter forced himself to sit down before he made a fool of himself by dancing the cha-cha-cha across the tiled floor. "Sorry. I didn't mean to make a scene. I'm just—" he paused, his voice trembling with laughter and disbelief, "just really happy."

Peter tried to come up with something more sophisticated to say, but all he could manage was the truth that he was really happy.

Sarah raised her hands as though she could hide her crimson face. "I should have waited somewhere more private," she murmured. "I'm sorry I didn't tell you sooner."

Peter grinned. "You loved me before now?"

Sarah's eyes glistened in the low light as she nodded. "Yes, of course I did. I just had a hard time telling you."

"Well, I loved you the first time I saw you. Not that I'm bragging or anything," Peter said as he puffed out his chest.

She shook her head. "There's no such thing as love at first sight."

"Au contraire, my little lovebird." Peter took her hand in his, feeling the softness of her skin against his palm. "When I saw you, it was love at first sigh."

"You mean first sight?"

"No, I mean sigh. I talked to SAUS about the subject, and we agreed that love at first sigh is a breath-catching exhale of instant romance. When I spotted your stunning beauty, I sighed in awe."

Sarah laughed. "I don't know whether to be flattered or insulted that you talked to AI about me."

Peter squeezed her hand. "Have no fear, my Salsa beauty. I realize true love is built on trust, commitment, shared experiences like amazing salsa, and intimacy like stolen kisses in the pantry."

"I hope you're not getting love advice from AI."

"No." He cringed. "Not much anyway. It's my job to work with AI, but for matters of the heart or anything dealing with real life, I talk to a higher power." He pointed up.

Sarah raised an eyebrow, her lips twitching in amusement. "I do hope you are pointing beyond the ceiling lights."

"Definitely. I need all the divine help I can get."

Chapter 23

Although Peter knew Quint didn't mind him staying as long as he wanted, Peter was ready to have his own place and get settled. Sneaking kisses with Sarah in different areas of Quint's house was entertaining, but having privacy would be much better.

Last night, Peter had searched online through real estate listings and narrowed his choices to four possibilities. One was a cabin not far out of town and close to neighbors. Two were new houses, and the last one was an older home in an established neighborhood.

He'd taken off the morning to meet with his realtor, Dallas Harlson. Fortunately, Dallas didn't try to influence Peter's decision. Instead, he let him explore each property at his own pace and without pressure.

After viewing his first choices, Peter knew the cabin wasn't for him, and the two new homes were nice but not what he wanted.

Dallas then drove the back roads, entered a well-maintained neighborhood with older homes, and stopped in the driveway of a one-story brick house.

As Peter got out of the car. He looked around, attempting to figure out his location. For some reason, the neighborhood seemed vaguely familiar. Then it hit him. Dot and Ulysses' house was on the next street.

Oh man, that would be great to be close to where Sarah was living. He tamped down his excitement. He needed to remember not to let that influence his decision.

Dallas opened the door and waited for Peter to enter. "The home has three generously sized bedrooms, two-and-a-half baths with a partially finished basement, and an oversized double car garage with ample storage. In addition, the house has hardwood floors, new windows throughout the upper level, new stainless steel kitchen appliances, and a covered deck. Plus, the area has a speedy fiber-optic network."

"Looks good, but I'll look around on my own."

"I'll be here if you have questions."

Peter went from room to room, looking, thinking, and praying. The home's price would easily fit within his income, and the size would provide enough bedrooms for sleeping, a home office, and space to host family members.

He returned to where Dallas was waiting. As they stepped out of the French doors onto the covered back deck, the gentle sound of wind chimes welcomed them. In the trees, birds sang, and a breeze cooled the warm morning.

Dallas's phone rang, and he stepped away to take his call.

Glancing at the sky, Peter sent up a silent prayer for help and wisdom. He didn't want to purchase another property without knowing for sure it was the place he needed to be. Only God knew where he belonged.

Peter strolled over the trimmed grass, paused at the rear fence, and then gazed back at the house. Flowers and neatly kept shrubs bordered the yard. The building's exterior, including the roof and siding, appeared to be in good condition.

Thanks to the covered deck, he could bring his laptop and work outside whenever he wanted. The lot was even big enough to justify buying a small riding lawnmower. Maybe he could even get a dog.

The house seemed ideal, but should he take the plunge? To

qualify for a reasonable home loan rate, he needed more funds than he had in his savings. Maybe he was rushing and should wait another month or two to save more money.

Peter ran his hand through his hair. He desperately needed divine guidance to know if this was the right place for him. Whispering another prayer, he made his way back inside.

While Dallas quietly continued talking on his cell phone, Peter stood in front of the family room's stone fireplace. If walls could talk, what would this house say? The home had a peaceful feeling, as though whoever owned it had loved it well. His realtor parents often talked about how houses frequently seemed to carry the personality of their owners—whether good or bad.

"I have good news," Dallas said as he walked toward Peter. "The owners are motivated to sell and willing to help with a down payment. The house is move-in ready."

"Seriously? That's great news." Peter stopped himself from getting too excited. Was that an answer to his prayers? "Wait. Before I decide, what do you know about the previous owners?"

"Mr. and Mrs. Williams had the house built and raised three kids. They're great people and were active in the community and church. Now that they're retired, they've moved to North Carolina, where their oldest son lives."

"How do you know all that?" Peter asked.

"I've lived here all my life and know them well," Dallas said. "Mr. Williams taught at the high school, and Mrs. Williams was a nurse at the doctor's office. And my grandmother and mother used to come here for Bible study every Tuesday night."

"That explains why the house feels well-loved and peaceful." Peter looked around, imagining a loving family and women studying the Bible together. Maybe if God blessed him, he could have a wife and children who would do the same.

"The house should be peaceful," Dallas continued. "Mr. and Mrs. Williams even prayed with me the day they listed the house, asking God that whoever bought it would be a good caretaker of the property. They also prayed for the new owner." Dallas's smile told Peter their prayers had been good ones.

His shoulders relaxing, Peter held out his hand. "I'll take it. I'm ready to sign the papers."

Busy with lunch preparation, Sarah stood at the restaurant grill, smoke curling around her and into the ventilation system.

While driving to work this morning, she'd spotted a white Lexus. Then, she'd seen a blonde-haired woman who looked like her mother going into the General Store. Was Heather in town? Sarah's stomach churned at the thought.

She whispered another silent prayer. *Please, God, don't let it be her.* She should have known that whenever her life was going well, something bad would happen.

So many times when she was a kid and finally settled at a school, Heather would move them to another place. Even as an adult, Sarah had her job taken away by a man she thought loved her.

The clatter of pans, the sizzle of the grill, and her sweet co-workers made the restaurant her home away from home. Then again, she was living in a house that didn't belong to her. Peter said he loved her, but he wasn't hers. Even in the restaurant, she was only an assistant chef. Nothing was permanent.

"Chef Sarah!" Grinning, Aaron called out as he walked toward her. "Clark Kent is here to see you." He motioned with his thumb toward the restaurant floor.

"Thank you." Her heart happy dancing in her chest, she

turned to Thomas. "Do you mind?"

"Not at all. Just don't be long. The orders are stacking up fast."

"I'll be back in a jiffy." Sarah took off her apron, laid it on a chair in the back, and made a quick check of her hair.

Hoping she was somewhat presentable, she hurried out the kitchen doors.

Spotting Peter staring at his phone as he munched on a chip, she walked toward him.

"Hey," Sarah slipped into the chair next to him.

It took a moment for Peter to look her way. "Hi. Sorry, I just got a message from work. SAUS is acting up."

"Do you need to go?"

He glanced again at his phone. "Yeah, but I have a few minutes." Peter took his hand in hers. "I just wanted to see you. Is your morning going well?"

"Yeah, it's okay." Other than being worried about her mother showing up again. Sarah tried to give Peter a smile she hoped would be pleasant. "We're swamped." Sarah motioned toward the tables full of customers.

"I noticed. I won't keep you. I have a question, though. What do you think of where Dot and Ulysses live? Is it a nice neighborhood?"

"It's great. The people are friendly, and everybody keeps up the houses. Why do you ask?"

"No special reason." Peter shrugged. "Are we still getting together Sunday?"

"Yes, I'll see you at church, and then we'll go to lunch."

"Great. I've got a surprise for you."

"Interesting. I look forward to seeing what you have in mind."

"Peter!" the attractive blonde-haired woman Sarah had

seen flirting with Peter at the town fair hurried toward him, her stiletto heels tapping on the floor. "How fun to see you here." She glanced at Sarah, her eyes narrowing a touch, before turning her overly flirty smile at Peter. "Are you heading back to the office?"

Peter's neck turned red as he nodded. "Yeah, AI emergency."

"Oh, silly SAUS. I'll see you later." With a wave of her manicured fingers, she turned and walked away, her hips swaying provocatively with each step.

Sarah stood. She knew it. Her good life had been flipped again to the bad side. "I'd better get back to the kitchen."

Peter got to his feet and leaned close. "I'd kiss you, but I wouldn't want to embarrass you."

The thought of his kiss brought a flutter of excitement, like happy butterflies, but she fought to maintain her composure. She couldn't take another heartbreak from a man who said one thing and did another. "I'll see you Sunday."

Sarah's tennis shoes squeaked as she turned to go, and she grimaced. High heels were out of the question for her job. Her fingernails were always clean, but she never wore seductive nail polish. She was only simple and plain.

Why would Peter want to stay with someone like her?

Sarah entered the kitchen and sent up a silent prayer for help to stop her negative thoughts.

Peter wasn't like her ex-boyfriend, and she wasn't the same person she'd been before. Sarah straightened her shoulders, put on her apron, and stood next to Thomas.

Between praying for God's help and praising God for Peter's love, Sarah imagined the grill's sizzling heat burning away her insecurities.

Chapter 24

"I tried not to let those things bother me, but insecurity attacked again." Sarah stood in Dot and Ulysses' kitchen, waiting for the decaf coffee to brew. "You wouldn't believe how that woman flirted with Peter right in front of me. She even gave me a dirty look."

"Sorry to say, but there are flirty women everywhere." Dot gave Sarah a compassionate look as she sipped her coffee.

"Well, they can flirt with someone other than Peter. And you know what else got me worried? I saw a white Lexus and a blonde-haired woman who looked like my mother. Is Heather in town to make me miserable?" Sarah didn't mean to keep complaining. She rubbed her eyes. Maybe she was just overly tired.

"Insecurity sure is a rabid monster," Dot said.

"I know, right?" Sarah poured coffee into her mug. "The monster has its claws firmly embedded in my mind. I did pretty well earlier today imagining my worries incinerating on the hot grill, but the later in the evening it got, the more I started worrying again."

"Exhausted individuals are easy targets for insecurity. As for your mother, according to Ulysses, Heather is still on a Caribbean island. From her whining social media posts, her latest lover left her there." Dot motioned for Sarah to follow her to the den.

"I'm sure she'll find someone else to latch onto." Sarah walked behind her aunt, then sat on the couch, a soft blanket draped across her lap. "Peter's such a nice guy, what would he want with someone like me?" Sarah stared into her dark coffee. Her stomach couldn't tolerate more acid. She set the cup on a coaster on the coffee table.

Dot put her feet up on the oversized coffee table in front of the couch. "Peter is with you because you're a wonderful, beautiful, kind, generous young woman. Besides the many things you do for us and at the restaurant, you don't give yourself enough credit. You've been kind and caring all your life. Remember the couple who lived next door when you came to visit when you were younger?"

"Yes, they were so fragile but very kind to me." Sarah felt some of the tension begin to drain from her shoulders at the memory of the elderly pair she wished had been her grandparents.

"And you were very kind to them," Dot said ."You cooked meals, enough to freeze for later, and you even helped clean their house. You didn't have to do any of those things, yet you jumped in to help lighten their load."

Sarah picked at a loose thread on the blanket on her lap. "I didn't do anything special."

"Maybe not in your eyes, but what you did blessed them more than you know." Dot pointed to the row of pictures on the fireplace mantle. "You also encouraged our youngest daughter so many times."

Sarah gazed at the photos. Dot and Ulysses's children were older than her, yet they'd made her feel part of their family. "I love you all. I'm grateful you let me stay when Heather dropped me off, since you didn't have much choice as she drove off and left me."

"We were thrilled whenever we got to be with you." Dot stood, went to the mantle, picked up a group of the famed photos, and placed them on the coffee table in front of Sarah. "We love having you with us. You're part of our family."

Sarah looked at the many photos of her at various ages alongside the other children, making it seem as if she'd always belonged with them. Unfortunately, her visits had never lasted long enough, and she'd have to go back with Heather to another city, another school, and another place where she never fit in.

"Who you are is a blessing to those you come in contact with," Dot said softly.

Sarah shrugged, her fingers absently running over the blanket's edge. "I doubt that. I'm just me and an ordinary nobody."

"Oh, my goodness, sweet girl. I wish you could see who you really are," Dot said. "That portrait Peter had the artist make of you as a princess is very accurate."

"I am *not* a princess."

"Yes, you are." Dot's gentle gaze rested on her. "Your father is a king."

"Yeah, right," Sarah scoffed. "I know that's not true." It was bad enough her father never wanted her; even worse, he was married to a woman who was not her mother. Her heart pounded as her mind flickered back to a night when she was a little girl alone in a creaky, unfamiliar house, listening for footsteps that never came.

"I'm talking about your true Father." Dot pointed toward the ceiling. "The correct and true perspective is that you are an eternally loved daughter of the King of kings."

Sarah pulled the blanket around her shoulders. Heather's harsh words, wishing she'd never been born, replayed in her mind. "I know you say that, but sometimes I wonder if I'm not worth loving."

"Oh, honey, that is *not* true." Dot reached over to squeeze

Sarah's hand. "You matter. You always have, and you always will. You're loved because of who you are, not just by us, but by God Himself."

Sarah wanted to believe that God loved her forever. She'd hoped before, sensed God's nearness, but every time it had been snatched away. The ache from her past pressing into the present, she shoved the cover off her as though its removal would ease her fears. "But what if Heather shows up again wanting money or just to make my life miserable? What if Peter runs off with another woman? What if the restaurant decides they don't need me? What if you both want your house to yourselves?"

"Sweet one," Dot placed her hand on Sarah's cheek, her touch soft and reassuring, grounding Sarah to the present. "If Heather does contact you again, you can stand firm knowing that God will help you in how to respond. I believe Peter and the restaurant love you."

Sarah leaned into her aunt's soft hand. "I don't want to keep feeling so anxious about every single thing that might go wrong."

"Oh, honey, with all your worrying about what might happen tomorrow, you're missing the blessings of today. Do you trust God?" Dot asked, her voice kind.

The rhythmic tick-tock of the clock on the mantle echoed through the room as though counting down until Sarah would answer.

Sarah drew in a shaky breath. Did she honestly trust God? "I think so. Maybe? I guess not as much as I should. It's just that anytime when my life was going well, something always happened that was bad."

"Always?" Dot gently prodded.

"Okay. Most times." Sarah cringed. "Sometimes."

Dot nodded. "I understand. When I was younger, I spent

too much time worrying and comparing myself to others. And I get very insecure every time we release a new book."

"Why? You're a best-selling author."

"That fact only makes me more anxious that our next book won't be as good as the others. However, I'm learning that our value isn't measured by who birthed us, what other people think, other people's choices, or fleeting feelings. Our worth is rooted in a love that never changes. God's love is forever. We love you, and God loves you, and that won't ever change."

Sarah squeezed the blanket tighter around her, wishing she could squeeze away her uncertainty. "All my life, I've wanted a mother and father to love me, and that never happened." Sarah took a shuddering breath. "And then when I met a man who said he loved me, instead, he betrayed me. Love is nothing more than a fleeting wish. You get a good day, then a bad one is going to hit you."

"When we expect something bad to happen," Dot said softly, "that's what we'll see and focus on. You noticed the flirty woman with Peter at the fair, forgetting it was you he was with. And when you saw her again at the restaurant, it was you that Peter came to see. *Not* her. As for the unfortunate issues with your mother, I wish I could change that, but you've survived. You got through, and you've become a wonderful woman with a wonderful career and life ahead of you. We love you, and God loves you too."

Sarah's heart fluttered, caught between gratitude and the ache of uncertainty. "But how do you know God loves me?" She wrung her hands, wishing she could wring away her past. "Even my mother and father don't want me."

"God doesn't love someone because they come from a good, loving family; He loves us no matter where we come from." Dot drew in a deep breath, her gaze locking onto Sarah.

"I know that true from my own experience, because I am the daughter of a prostitute."

Sarah's world lurched, her breath snagging in her chest as shock rippled through her. The familiar shapes of the cozy room seemed to shift and blur; the soft glow of the lamp, the scent of Dot's perfume, everything felt distant, surreal. "But... I thought loving parents raised you. I remember seeing family pictures."

Dot gave a gentle smile. "Those were photos of my adopted family. At five, I entered foster care, and at eight, I was given my new family."

Trying to keep from sobbing, Sarah leaned over, her body shaking. "I'm so sorry. I didn't know." How could she have spent all that time complaining about her life when Dot had been through much worse? "I'm so sorry."

Dot put her arm around Sarah's shoulders while she cried. "Shhh, it's okay. Only a few people know — Ulysses and our children, which includes you."

Sarah stared at her aunt. "But that means my mother isn't really your relative."

"That's correct. Heather is related to the family who raised me."

"And you still took me in?"

"Of course. We're family, not by blood, but through a loving bond. All our children were adopted, some at birth, others from foster care."

Sarah gasped. "How can that be? You all look alike." She'd seen baby photos and pictures from when the kids were all younger.

Dot smiled. "It's funny how God worked that out."

"I can't thank you enough for how kind you've been to me."

"You are our daughter. We've claimed you. You were in and out of our lives when you were younger, but you're here now, and you'll always be in our hearts."

Sarah laid her hand on Dot's. "I'm not going anywhere."

"Good. Now, sweet one, even on days when you doubt yourself, or when the world seems determined to make you feel small, remember that you are cherished. Not just by us but by the King of kings. And that makes you a princess, no matter what anyone else says."

Dot pulled Sarah to her feet and wrapped her arms around her. "You're loved, you belong, and you are a blessing. Now, flick that insecurity off your shoulders and enjoy the life God has given you."

Sarah held tight to the woman who opened her heart and home. Something inside her eased, loosened. She didn't really believe she was a princess, but now, in this moment, she knew she was forever loved.

Chapter 25

Sarah stood as the praise team began the final song. Being with Peter at church made the music sound sweeter and the sermon more heartfelt. Or maybe the truth was she felt it more in her heart after her conversation with Dot a few weeks ago.

Plus, she'd finally confided in Peter about her upbringing and the difficulties she had with her mother. Fortunately, he'd been kind and understanding, even though he admitted he couldn't imagine what she'd been through since he'd had a happy childhood.

Sarah sent up silent prayers of thanks for the many blessings in her life. Insecurity would probably attack at times, but now she felt stronger, more able to handle that rabid monster.

Once the service was over, Peter reached for her hand and gave her fingers a gentle squeeze. "That was a great service. I like a message that points out areas I need to work on."

"You probably don't have any areas like that."

"Seriously? You know better than that. My issues have issues with their issues."

Sarah grinned and nudged him with her shoulder. "There's no point in arguing about that issue."

Peter snorted a chuckle as they joined the gentle tide of people flowing toward the church doors. The cool fall air swirled around them as the sun warmed Sarah's face when they stepped outside. The light breeze carried the scent of fallen leaves and wood smoke.

Children's laughter rang out as they darted in and out, playing chase as adults mingled, and clusters of teenagers stood together talking and laughing.

As they made their way across the lot, Dot and Ulysses smiled and waved. Sarah and Peter returned the greeting.

Once they reached his Jeep, Peter opened the passenger-side door and waited until Sarah buckled in. Once in the driver's seat, he turned toward her. "You don't get carsick, do you?"

Sarah shot him a curious look. "No."

"Good." Peter started his vehicle and handed her a blindfold. "Would you mind putting this on?"

Sarah's eyebrows shot up in surprise. "Here? Now?"

Through the windshield, sunlight glinted off rows of cars in the bustling church parking lot. "Good point. I'll tell you when to put it on."

"Why?"

"I want to surprise you with something." Peter drove out of the church parking lot, through downtown, then followed the curvy road lined with fall's vibrant maple trees. "Would you mind putting it on now, please?"

She gave him a look that said she was wary but curious. "Okay, fine. But keep your hands on the steering wheel. I expect you to be a gentleman."

"Yes, ma'am. I promise." Peter turned into the neighborhood and parked in the driveway of the house that was soon to be his. He leaned over and kissed Sarah's cheek. "Wait until I come to get you." He hurried around to her side. "I'll help you walk for a few steps, then when you're in position, you can take off the blindfold."

Sarah placed her hand in his as Peter led her to the sidewalk. Dallas had given him the key so he could show Sarah the house he was buying.

Peter lined her up to get the best view. As he stood next to Sarah, he wondered if he'd done the right thing. What if she didn't like the house? What if their relationship progressed to the serious stage, and she wanted to buy a house together or build one?

"Peter?" Sarah reached out to find him.

"Oh, sorry. Okay. You can take off the blindfold."

She blinked a few times as the sunlight hit her eyes. "What am I looking at?"

"My new house."

"Yours?" Sarah's eyes widened in surprise as she took in the house and yard.

"Yes. I mean, I'm buying it and will close at the end of the month." With a prayer for good results, Peter unlocked the door and stepped aside to let her enter. "What do you think?"

"Oh, Peter, it's really nice." Sarah walked through the family room and paused at the stone fireplace." She turned to him. "The house almost feels peaceful. If that makes sense."

"Yeah, it does." His knees almost went weak with relief that she seemed pleased. "You know what else? It's only a street away from where you live."

Sarah smiled. "So, that's why you were asking about our neighborhood."

"Yep. And now you have one more friendly neighbor." He kissed her. "But you better not be that friendly with anyone else in the neighborhood or anywhere else."

"I promise. Having you so close is exciting. No more hiding in the pantry. We're free to kiss at any time." She smiled in a way that sent his heart racing.

"Yes, we can. But before I do something I'll regret, how about I show you around?"

Peter watched as Sarah's eyes widened, taking in every detail as he led her through the house. "Do you like it?"

"I really do. It's very nice."

Peter took her hand in his. "I'll probably have the kitchen redone to bring it up-to-date. Do you have any ideas?"

"It's fine as it is, but I don't know. It's your house."

"I would really appreciate your help. How would you do it if the house were yours?"

A look of longing crossed Sarah's face as her gaze moved around the kitchen area. "I'm not sure."

"How would Chef Sarah change the kitchen?"

"Well, a chef would make some pretty major adjustments."

Peter wrapped his arms around her and drew her close. "I would be very grateful if you would design my kitchen renovation to create the perfect space for a chef."

Sarah gazed up at him. "I would be honored and totally enjoy doing that for you."

"Good. One final request. How about we seal that promise with a kiss?" Peter was not disappointed with her sweet, demonstrative reply.

Chapter 26

Peter's nervous hands trembled as he stared at himself in the mirror and straightened his tie. He hadn't worn one in years, but he wanted tonight to be special. After combing his hair, he checked his blazer coat pocket. Yep, he was ready to go.

He made a quick pass through the house, checking that everything was clean and in place. He stopped in his brand-new, redesigned kitchen, made perfect for a chef by the perfect chef he was dating. Sarah hadn't seen the finished product yet, and he couldn't wait to see what she thought.

Peter peeked into the brand-new oven. The aroma of steak and baked potatoes curled around him. He couldn't take credit for any part of the meal, since he'd purchased the dinner from the steakhouse. There was no way he would have cooked something special for tonight. The new refrigerator kept the salad, dessert, and sweet iced tea cold, so he was about ready.

Fortunately, Dot had come over earlier to help him with the planning and set the table with her China and silverware.

Peter checked the time on his phone. He had ten minutes before he needed to leave to pick up Sarah.

Crossing to the entry closet, he slid out the gift set aside for tonight. Where should he place it? If he put the gift on the mantle, he'd need to hide it under something. He didn't want to leave it in the closet, and he didn't want Sarah to see it until the proper time.

He scanned his family room. His big-screen television displayed a video of beautiful scenery as soft music played from the speakers. Besides his sofa, one of his chairs had a blanket draped over it. Perfect. He'd hide the gift on the chair under the cover.

Peter sent up a prayer for help and hurried to his Jeep.

"Ouch!" Sarah grimaced as Dot worked to put Sarah's hair up in a fancy bun. "Is this necessary?"

"Yes," Dot said. "You need to look your best."

"Just where is Peter taking me that I have to get so dressed up? Garden Valley has only one steakhouse, and they aren't this fancy."

"It's a surprise," Dot giggled.

Her aunt wasn't one to giggle. Although Sarah wanted to roll her eyes, she was having a good time looking glamorous. She was wearing a fancy dress, high heels, and nail polish, all because Dot insisted she buy them.

"All done," Dot stepped back and smiled, her eyes teary-eyed. "You look so beautiful."

Sarah stood and gazed at her reflection in the mirror. The shimmering dress fit her as if it were made just for her. Showing off her curves was an odd experience. Goodness, she didn't know she could look this curvy, especially since most of her days she was draped in an apron as she worked in the restaurant kitchen.

The doorbell rang. "I'll get it," Ulysses called from the other room.

The murmur of voices came from the entry.

Dot hugged Sarah tight. "Now, go enjoy your evening."

"I will." Nervous, excited, and curious about what the evening might bring, Sarah attempted a graceful exit, but instead stumbled in her high heels. So much for her attempts at being sexy. She took a deep breath and tried to walk in a glamorous manner.

Sarah stepped into the family room, where Peter stood talking with Ulysses. The dark-blue blazer jacket Peter was wearing highlighted his shoulders and slim waist.

"Wow!" Peter's mouth dropped open for a moment as his appreciative gaze swept over her. "You look amazing."

"You look mighty fine yourself, Mr. Edwards." She focused on walking gracefully as she moved toward him.

He crooked his arm. "May I escort you to my waiting chariot?"

"I would be honored, kind sir." Sarah glanced at where her aunt and uncle stood, teary-eyed as if she'd won a beauty contest. "Don't wait up."

Peter guided Sarah to his Jeep, opened her door, and waited until she was settled and buckled in, then hurried to his side.

"So, where are we going?"

Peter started the engine and grinned. "Sit back and relax."

"Is it that far?"

He chuckled. "You'll see."

A few minutes later, he pulled into the driveway of the house he had bought.

Sarah gave him a curious look. "Why are we stopping here?"

"I want to show you something." Peter led her inside. Soft music played on his television, and tantalizing smells drifted from his kitchen.

Excitement bubbling, Sarah turned to Peter. "Is it finished?"

He grinned as he took her hand and led her into the renovated kitchen.

She squealed in delight at the sight of the gas six-burner stove with double ovens. Quartz countertops gleamed, paired with the warmth of stunning kitchen cabinets. "Oh, Peter, it's beautiful."

"All thanks to my beautiful designer. Would you care to dine with me this evening?" Peter gestured toward the table, where fine china gleamed under the golden glow of a candelabra, the silverware catching the soft flicker of the flames.

"Have a seat, and I will serve you, my lady." Peter stepped behind Sarah and pulled out her chair. As she sat, he leaned close and pressed a gentle kiss to her neck, sending a shiver of delight down her spine.

Moments later, Peter placed a salad, steak, and a baked potato on the table. He took his seat across from her and extended his hand across the table. "Mind if I pray?" he asked softly.

Feeling as if she were living a dream, Sarah slid her fingers into his and closed her eyes.

Peter's words, gentle and heartfelt, wrapped around her like a cozy blanket, each phrase infusing her with peace and a sense of belonging.

As they ate and savored the meal and dessert, they talked and laughed about their time together and how much fun they'd had. The candlelight danced in Peter's eyes as he watched her, his smile warm and genuine.

The meal finished, Peter rose, a nervous excitement flickering across his face. "I have a surprise for you."

"You've surprised me enough. I've already had a wonderful evening."

"It's just starting." Peter led her to the couch and invited her to sit.

As she settled in, the softness of the cushions cradled her, adding to the dreamy atmosphere.

Peter stood in front of her. "Sarah Livingstone, you are the most amazing, beautiful woman I've ever known. I hope this makes you smile." Crossing to his chair, he removed a blanket.

Sarah gasped, her breath catching at the sight of a vivid portrait of her as a regal princess and Peter at her side as a prince. The portrait's colors shimmered in the soft light, as though the fantasy was real.

She turned to him, heart pounding, just as Peter dropped to one knee.

He opened a velvet box, the deep blue lining making the princess-cut diamond sparkle like a star. "Sarah Livingstone, I'm not a prince and can't offer you a kingdom or a castle, but I promise to love you forever. Will you marry me?"

Overwhelmed with emotion, Sarah pressed a trembling hand to her mouth. For a heartbeat, she was speechless, her breath catching with joy and disbelief. "Yes, Peter—absolutely yes!"

He jumped to his feet and swept her into his arms, holding her close as if he never wanted to let go.

As they kissed, Sarah's lips tingled, overflowing with happiness until she was sure they were swollen and smiling with pure delight.

The music wrapped around them as Peter held her close. They swayed to the melody, moving in perfect time as though professional ballroom dancers. The moment felt as magical as the promise she'd just made to become his wife.

His hand rested gently at the small of her back, guiding her as they spun together, their laughter mixing with the soft notes of the music.

The room seemed to fade away, leaving only the warmth of

his embrace. Sarah felt safe and cherished as they moved in perfect harmony.

Peter twirled Sarah, pulling her close again until she could feel the steady beat of his heart against her own. He leaned in, his lips brushing her ear. "I had you design the kitchen because I hoped someday you'd enjoy it as my wife."

What a sweet surprise, but she couldn't resist teasing him. "Oh, so you only want to marry me for my cooking skills?"

He pressed a gentle kiss to her neck, lingering for a heartbeat. The touch sent a shiver down her spine, and she melted further into his embrace.

"I'd marry you if you couldn't even boil water," he murmured. "Of course, you are the total package. Brains, beauty, and an amazing cook."

"So, what do I get with you, Peter Edwards?" she teased.

He drew her even closer, their bodies swaying together as one. "Hmm. I can code and work with AI."

She laughed as he spun her again and brought her back into his arms. "I don't know. It's going to take a lot of faith to jump into a marital relationship with you."

Peter met her gaze with a smile full of promise. "You cook, I'll code, and we'll take a leap of faith."

Epilogue

Ulysses shot out of his chair. "Beautiful wedding!"

Sarah forced her mouth closed as she stared at her uncle. "That isn't the answer."

"The game *is* Charades," Dot said with an attempt at an innocent smile.

Sarah playfully narrowed her eyes at her aunt and uncle. "You're supposed to guess the words and not make up your own." She turned to her sweet husband of four weeks. "Isn't there a rule about this?"

Peter grinned. "I'm not getting into this argument." He drew her closer as they sat on the couch in their family room. "However, if you agree to a kiss, I might see what I can do."

Sarah gave him a sly grin and planted a humongous kiss on his lips.

Her husband gave a nervous chuckle. "Thank you, Mrs. Edwards. Thank you very much."

"You're more than welcome, Mr. Edwards."

"Okay, you two get a room." Dot grinned with a shake of her head. "Now, back to our words." Dot rose gracefully, as if ready to command the stage. "You, Sarah Livingstone, looked radiant, like a dream, at your beautiful wedding. The sun's rays through the church windows showcased your exquisitely styled hair." Dot's voice rose with a dramatic flair. "As your eyes stayed focused on the one you love, your skin seemed to radiate with an inner light."

Ulysses stood next to his wife while his mischievous gaze

stayed on Sarah. "You were a princess floating down the church aisle, the fabric of your gown whispering with each step."

"And Peter," Dot playfully nudged Ulysses to move over. "wearing his dashing charcoal tuxedo, looked at you with starry eyes, knowing deep down that Sarah Livingstone was the most gorgeous, incredible woman in the world and would soon be his bride."

Sarah laughed. "You both are too much."

"We are authors." Dot's eyebrows playfully wiggled.

"Good thing you don't use over-the-top prose in your mystery novels."

"That's for sure. However, it is fun at times to let the words fly with abandon."

Ulysses motioned with his chin toward Peter. "I thought he was going to pass out when you entered the church."

"I almost did. Sarah took my breath away." Peter gave her a look that still curled her toes in happiness.

Sarah grinned at her husband. "Quint told me later he wished he'd brought a paper bag, so you didn't hyperventilate."

"It did take me a while to be able to breathe as you walked toward me." Peter nuzzled her neck.

Sarah giggled and sighed at the wonderful memories. They had planned a quiet ceremony with only a few people, but as soon as they set the date, Peter's work friends wanted to come, and the entire restaurant staff and a few of their customers, and more townspeople than Sarah could count, had joined in. It seemed the majority of Garden Valley had been there.

She closed her eyes, and the memory of Ulysses walking her down the aisle flooded back, along with the scent of flowers and Dot's wide, tear-filled smile. Peter's family, whom Sarah adored from the moment they met, had greeted her with open arms and more hugs than she'd had in her lifetime. Ulysses and

Dot's children and grandchildren were all there too, filling what seemed like ten rows in the church.

As a wedding present, Dot and Ulysses had gifted Sarah with adoption papers. She was now officially a member of their family.

And best of all, Peter was hers. Sarah sent a silent prayer of thanks up to God, then snuggled into her husband's arms.

She was now Sarah Livingstone Franks Edwards, and she was finally home.

The end

of the story and the beginning of Peter
and Sarah's happily ever after.

Thank you for reading

Cook, Code, and a Leap of Faith

Acknowledgments

Thank You, Father God, for Your kindness and compassion. Thank You for providing healing and restoration for wounded hearts and the blessings of Your forever family.

Dennis, thank you for being a loving, wonderful husband. Thank you for your prayers, support, encouragement, and the innumerable bowls of salsa you have purchased for me over the years. I sure am grateful we're together.

Patricia (Pacjac) Carroll, thank you again for the helpful feedback and for making the writing process enjoyable.

JoAnn Durgin, thank you for creating another beautiful cover. You are a sweet blessing to me and so many others.

Readers, thank you for taking the time to read *Cook, Code, and a Leap of Faith.* I hope you liked Sarah and Peter's story. If you enjoyed the novel, would you be so kind as to leave a positive review and share it with friends? Thank you.

Please visit Lisa at https://lisabuffaloe.com
Facebook https://facebook.com/lisabuffaloe
Twitter (X) https://x.com/lisabuffaloe
Instagram https://instagram.com/buffaloelisa
Amazon https://amzn.to/4ltfEBA

About the Author

Lisa Buffaloe is a happily married mom, speaker, and multi-published author. She loves spending time with God, her sweet hubby, studying the Bible, writing, and enjoying nature.

Please visit Lisa at https://lisabuffaloe.com
Facebook https://facebook.com/lisabuffaloe
Twitter (X) https://x.com/lisabuffaloe
Instagram https://instagram.com/buffaloelisa
Amazon https://amzn.to/4ltfEBA

Books by Lisa

Fiction

Garden Valley Series

Each novel may be enjoyed separately or as part of the series.

Clues, Crushes, and Second Chances
Cook, Code, and a Leap of Faith

Crawdad Beach Series

The novels may be enjoyed separately or as part of the series.

Visible, yet Hidden   *Mia Lets Go*
Running to Grace   *A New Paige*
Crystal's Journey Home   *Running from Shame*
A Baker's Heart   *Elise's New Song*
Stella's Heart Code   *A Found Joy*
River Steps Free   *A Healing Rain*

Hope and Grace Series

Each novel may be enjoyed separately or as part of the series.

Nadia's Hope   *The Discovery Chapter*
Prodigal Nights   *Open Lens*
Writing Her Heart

Stand-alone novels

The Masterpiece Beneath
The Fortune
Grace for the Char-Baked

Non-Fiction

Finding Freedom in a Binding World
Float by Faith
Heart and Soul Medication
Time with The Timeless One
The Forgotten Resting Place
Present in His Presence
We Were Meant for Paradise
One Lit Step: Devotions for your journey
The Unnamed Devotional
Flying on His Wings
Unfailing Treasures
No Wound Too Deep For The Deep Love of Christ
Living Joyfully Free Devotional (Volumes 1 & 2)

Cook, Code, and a Leap of Faith

Lisa Buffaloe

www.ingramcontent.com/pod-product-compliance
Lightning Source LLC
Chambersburg PA
CBHW071521170626
46811CB00007B/2925